In the Service of Satan

Colin Diyen

Langaa Research & Publishing CIG
Mankon, Bamenda

Publisher:
Langaa RPCIG
Langaa Research & Publishing Common Initiative Group
P.O. Box 902 Mankon
Bamenda
North West Region
Cameroon
Langaagrp@gmail.com
www.langaa-rpcig.net

Distributed in and outside N. America by African Books Collective
orders@africanbookscollective.com
www.africanbookcollective.com

ISBN: 9956-791-56-3

DISCLAIMER
All views expressed in this publication are those of the author and do not necessarily reflect the views of Langaa RPCIG.

Dedication

Benjamin Tosangeng Diyen has not been reading my books. I want him to make a special effort on this one.

My sons, Ndam Edmond Nkehachia and Ndam Celestin Diyen are expected to enjoy this story very well.

1

Mr. Bzinkem was a very a rich man. He lived quite lavishly in a high standing villa located in the high class neighbourhood of the city. To make his life quite comfortable, he employed a driver, a cook, a housekeeper, and a yard boy. His safety at home was ensured by an expensive security company that watched his house around the clock. He lived in Mbongkesu, the capital of the country.

His acquaintances imagined him to be around sixty or sixty-five years of age. He was still quite handsome and attractive to women, but there was no open display of frivolity where women were concerned. Bzinkem drank moderately, was a fervent Christian, and gave freely to the church. His lavish support to the church, his considerable support to charity, and his lavish donations during fundraising occasions earned him additional respect.

Bzinkem was an actual example of a gentleman, and in the eyes of every one, lived up to it. But there was another side to Bzinkem of which nobody was aware and which was shaded by his neat outward appearance, gentlemanly behaviour, and generosity. Bzinkem had moved into the neighbourhood seven years ago and nobody actually knew from where he had come. He had bought the opulent villa where he still lived. His affluence was quite evident, but his actual source of income was not quite clear. He spent three days each week away from his home, but nobody knew where he disappeared to. There was equally the issue of his age. His external appearance had virtually not changed since he came to Mbongkesu despite the seven years that had gone by. Mr

Bzinkem was such a model gentleman that nobody bothered to question anything that seemed odd about him.

As Mr Bzinkem stepped out of his club one Friday afternoon and moved to his car, he felt a slight pain in his chest. That was the signal. It was time to rejuvenate. He told the driver he felt like driving himself and asked him to go home.

"I have a serious discussion with a friend and will certainly pass the night there," Bzinkem told the driver. "So pass through the house and tell everybody to go home."

This was not unusual. Occasions like this had occurred before where he had decided to spend the night at a friend's and sent all of them home early. On such occasions, only the watchmen stayed on, lodged in their small booth near the gate but no access to the inside of the villa.

"Thank you, sir," the driver replied as Bzinkem handed over money for the taxi. The amount was enough to enable the driver pay his taxi fare home, stand several rounds of drinks to his friends, and still have some change.

"You people don't need to come early tomorrow. I will have breakfast at my friend's before coming home," Bzinkem said.

"That is alright, sir," the driver answered and left.

Drivers and servants always look forward to such impromptu holidays, and as usual, the driver had been given enough money to have a good time during the free day. Bzinkem had investigated and found out that the driver was quite generous; he gave drinks to his colleagues from the unexpected windfall each time.

Bzinkem watched the driver go and then, starting the vehicle, drove to a posh snack bar where he sat for thirty minutes over a Gin Campari. As he sipped his drink slowly, he calculated his next move. He needed a motor park or a bus station where he could locate a visitor, male and of about thirty five years. The age range between thirty and forty was alright. Mbongkesu was quite a large town and had four motor parks from which you could take off to different parts of the country, and Bzinkem had already had victims from all of them before. There were also bus stations that belonged to the various travelling agencies, and some of them were quite busy. Bzinkem decided to try one of them and reserve the motor parks for bigger deals.

After finishing his drink, Bzinkem stepped out of the snack bar and strode to his car. He was a very neat man, and each time he approached his car, he examined it for any specks of dust or stain of mud. The car was quite clean. He entered the car, started the engine, and drove off to the big bus station he had decided on. Parking the vehicle at a strategic point, he watched as passengers alighted from a bus that had just arrived from some far-off destination. He soon spotted a young man of about thirty-seven years and decided that he had found what he was looking for. The young man was well dressed and looked neat. As the capital city of the country, Mbongkesu was always flooded with strangers coming in from other towns for one transaction or another. Bzinkem came out of the car and moved up to him.

"Excuse me," Bzinkem said, "may I talk to you for a second?"

"It's alright, sir," the young man answered. "How may I help you?"

"Are you from this town, or you are coming in as a stranger?" Bzinkem asked.

"I live and work in this town," the man said. "I simply travelled out on mission."

Bzinkem was unfortunate. He needed a stranger.

"That is good," he said untruthfully. "Could you then direct me to Boyo hotel?"

"That is easy, sir," the young man said. "Are you going by taxi or have you your own car?"

"My car is parked over there," Bzinkem said, pointing.

"That makes it easier," the man said. "When you drive out of here, turn left, then drives to the big roundabout some three hundred meters from here. Turn left again and drive on for about five hundred meters. You will see it on your right. "

"Thank you very much," Bzinkem said, moving back to his car.

He climbed in and sat down, and continued watching for another arriving bus

After about twenty five minutes, another bus arrived full of passengers. Bzinkem watched closely as they alighted, hoping that this time a vulnerable stranger would be among them. The bus brought in many people, ranging from elderly men and women to young men and women to children. There were a few that seemed of the required age, but they all seemed to be accompanied by some blasted female or friends.

The next bus looked more promising; and, as Bzinkem watched, he identified about three of the arriving passengers to be between thirty and forty years of age. He concentrated on one of them, a young man dressed in jeans. He was waiting for some luggage of his to be brought down from the carriage. Bzinkem waited for the man to retrieve his luggage, then stepped out of the car and went up to him.

"Can I talk to you for a moment?" he asked.

"Sure," the man replied.

"Do you live in this town or you are just visiting?" Bzinkem asked.

"I live far away in Konene town," the young man replied.

"Ah, you live in Konene," Bzinkem said. "And what has brought you all the way to Mbongkesu?"

"I have a problem with my salary," the man said. "I came down to follow up and have things rectified."

"You did not come to visit friends or relatives then," Bzinkem said, satisfied.

"No," the young man said, "I came here to follow up on some documents that I sent but have not had any reply to."

"You are a stranger in this town then?" Bzinkem said.

"Yes," the man replied.

"Where do you plan to stay? In a hotel? Or do you have a welcoming friend?" Bzinkem asked.

"I intend to get a cheap hotel for the night. I don't have that much money," the man said.

"Let me take you to my home first and show you why I came up to you." Bzinkem said "You are certainly wondering why I should walk up to a total stranger and start asking questions. I hope you don't have anything else to do now?"

"No!" said the visitor. " I simply had to look for an affordable hotel, have a bite, take a beer or two and retire for the day. "

"That is okay then." said Bzinkem. "There is enough in my house to eat and lots to drink. That is my car over there. "

They both moved to the car and got in.

"My name is Wainchom." said Bzinkem "May I know yours?"

"Ngangdi," the stranger said, "NyongoNgangdi."

Bzinkem drove carefully, relieved that he had found a victim without much headache. At times he went through

5

more than five incoming buses before finding the right man. His victims had to be of the male sex and fall within an age range of between thirty and forty.

They drove up to Bzinkem's villa and the gate was opened by one of the day watchmen. These would soon go away to be replaced by night watchmen who would have no idea whether Bzinkem was in there with anybody. Bzinkem lived alone in the big house. He neither had a wife nor children. He did not even seem to have any relatives. It was rumoured that his wife and children all died in some ghastly accident, compelling him to move away from the town where they had been living.

It never even occurred to the guards that, on certain rare occasions, he was seen driving in with a visitor or two but that these visitors were never seen leaving.

"You have good taste, sir, and class," Ngangdi said, admiring the beautiful villa and expensive cars parked within the gate.

"We try to live, my son," Bzinkem said. "But what is the use of all these when you are alone?"

"You live alone here?" the stranger asked. "In this big house that can comfortably take more than ten adults?"

"I have servants, about five of them, but they all work and go back home, leaving me all alone at night."

"You don't have family?" Ngangdi asked as they entered the living room. "Not even distant relatives?"

"My wife died five years ago," Bzinkem said. "Now come across here and look at this picture."

"But that is me," Ngangdi said. "That is exactly me, only I have never owned that kind of expensive suit he is putting on."

"Yes, the resemblance is really striking," Bzinkem said. "I hope you have now realized why I came up to you when I saw you at the bus station."

"But who is he?" Ngangdi asked.

"That is my son," Bzinkem answered. "My only son. God gives and God takes. "

"What do you mean?" Ngangdi asked.

"He is dead and gone," Bzinkem said. "He died in a ghastly car accident alongside his wife and two children. He was driving. "

Ngangdi would never know that the portrait picture of the supposed son of Bzinkem always adjusted to the image of the victim standing in front of it.

"I am sorry, sir," Ngangdi said.

"I have gone through a lot of pain and loneliness," Bzinkem said sadly. "I am the youngest and last of my two sisters and brother. I worked most of my life out of the country as a senior diplomat so I have not made friends back home. "

"That is quite sad, sir," Ngangdi said.

"Please, call me Daddy," Bzinkem said. "Would you accept to be my son?"

"How, sir?" Ngangdi asked/

"I don't expect that you should change your names and give up your biological father. Just keep calling me Dad and visiting me often. You see, there is a lot to inherit here and no family member in line. "

Ngangdi thought fast. His annual income was small and he was heavily indebted. Maybe he had stumbled across a solution at last.

"If you have any financial problems, I am there to help you," Bzinkem continued. "That is a father's role."

Ngangdi smiled. God had heard his prayers at last.

"By the way, can you drive?" Bzinkem asked.

"Yes, Dad. I had a rickety car which is now broken down. But I can drive very well," Ngangdi said.

"Well," Bzinkem said. "As you can see, there are several cars outside. You could use one tomorrow for your movement in town and even take it back with you. "

"Take it back with me? My gratitude knows no bounds, sir," Ngangdi said.

"You remind me very much of my son and you have accepted to replace him," Bzinkem said. "All I have will soon be yours. I am no longer a young man."

"But still, sir, your generosity is beyond expectation. I am a very lucky man, sir," Ngangdi said.

"Yes, and I will show even more generosity as we get along," Bzinkem said. "I shall start today. I will show you your room where you will sleep tonight instead of going to some flea-infested hotel. Each time you come visiting, the room will be available to you. "

"Thank you, Dad," Ngangdi said happily.

"And the servants," Bzinkem said. "You have full command over them. This is now your home, you know? You are second in command here. "

"I am very grateful, Dad," Ngangdi said.

"Ah, and you must be hungry. Go to the kitchen and serve yourself to anything you want. There are drinks in that cupboard over there and chilled beer in the kitchen. "

As Ngangdi stood up and went to the kitchen to serve himself, Bzinkem smiled happily. His usual bait of presenting enticing prospects of wealth and a beautiful car had worked wonderfully. The young man had taken the bait like a hungry and careless fish.

8

Ngangdi came back with a heaped plate and sat down to eat. Not being used to the habit of eating with wine, he had opted for a can of beer.

"Bon appetite, my son," Bzinkem said.

"Merci, papa," Ngangdi answered.

Bzinkem watched the young man eating for a while and then stood up.

"As I said, there is enough beer. There are whiskeys, cognac, vermouth, and other drinks in the cupboard there. Have your pick. I wish to go in and change, then I will come and show you your room. "

Ngangdi ate happily, finished his beer, and decided to inspect the cupboard full of assorted drinks.

There were different types of expensive table wines and port wines. Among the other drinks he could only recognize Martini and Campari because they were common and popular. He was surprised to find whiskeys with green, blue and gold labels. He had only been used to red and black. He decided to go back to the beer that he was acquainted with.

Bzinkem came back to the living room and led Ngangdi to a room not far off.

"Bring along your suitcase," Bzinkem said. "You will find towels and pyjamas in the room. If you need anything, just let me know. "

Ngangdi went in and kept his bag. He spent ten minutes simply admiring the room and finally went back to the living room and to his beer.

"Did your son need to work when he was alive?" Ngangdi asked.

"Actually, he did not need to but he insisted on having a career and earning his own money," Bzinkem replied. "What I have could have been quite enough for everybody though."

"How come he looks so much like me?" Ngangdi asked. "Are you sure you are not my real father, too?"

"I used to be a philanderer in my young days but I wonder whether I could have strayed to your mother." Bzinkem said "My class was quite high and besides, I worked mostly out of the country."

"And my biological father could never have had any access to your wife," Ngangdi said.

"No way," Bzinkem said. "My wife was very class conscious and reserved,"

"How come you don't have any relations around?" Ngangdi asked. "There are always distant uncles, aunts, cousins, nieces or nephews who would gladly want to attach themselves to a generous rich man like you."

"In my family, I was close only to my direct brothers and sisters and they are all dead," Bzinkem said. "Their children are all out of the country making so much money on their own that my wealth means nothing to them."

"And the distant ones?"

"As for the distant ones, I have never met them and they are all very scared of coming anywhere near me."

"Should I serve you something to drink, Dad?" Ngangdi was already fitting in properly.

"I think I will have cognac," Bzinkem said. "Get a bottle of Courvoisier from the cupboard and a glass from that shelve."

Ngangdi brought the cognac and the glass and placed them in front of Bzinkem.

"Thank you, son," Bzinkem said.

An appetizer before the real feast. Bzinkem was a real friend, but those who had fallen in his trap had never lived to reveal it. He smiled happily as he observed Ngangdi filling himself up with beer and wallowing in the abundance offered by Bzinkem. The last super? If only he knew what awaited him that night.

Bzinkem drank very slowly. He had to remain lucid enough for the night's feast. Yet he had to keep Ngangdi company as a drinking partner till it was time to retire to bed. While drinking, they followed a football match over TV and later on switched over to a soap opera. Ngangdi was quite relaxed and conversation flowed between them as if they had known each other for years. By nine p. m. however, Bzinkem declared that it was time to sleep, wished Ngangdi a good night's sleep, and went off to his room. Ngangdi stayed on for a short while, finished a last can of beer, and retired to his room. The bed was quite comfortable and the sheets looked very expensive. After changing into his pyjamas and brushing his teeth, Ngangdi switched off the TV in the room before climbing into bed. He was already drowsy and it did not take him long to fall into a deep sleep.

Deep in the night, Ngangdi suddenly got up perspiring profusely. He had been dreaming that a huge serpent with hands and looking very much like Mr Bzinkem was inserting the needle of a huge syringe into his throat and extracting blood. With dazed eyes he thought he was actually seeing Mr Bzinkem, only instead of a syringe, he was holding a long ugly knife. Ngangdi blinked and looked again. It was actually Mr Bzinkem only this time his face was contorted into a horrid leer. He looked like a true fiend as he thrust the knife into Ngangdi's chest around the heart and started cutting.

11

Ngangdi attempted to shout but could not. All efforts to move were in vain. He must have been drugged, he thought. It was then that he noticed the syringe with a bloody needle lying on his stomach. It must have been used to inject something into him that would render him inactive.

Mr Bzinkem kept on cutting and the pain was excruciating. As Ngangdi's vision became blurred, he noticed Mr Bzinkem applying his lips on the open wound and sucking blood. Then he passed out.

Mr Bzinkem continued his macabre operation and cut open the area covering the heart. He dipped his two hands inside and brought out the warm heart. It had to be eaten warm. He held the heart up, smacked his bloody lips and raised his voice in invocation of some higher being.

"Oh great one, master of all evil," he chanted in a guttural voice. "Accept this offering and shower your favour unto me, thy servant. I am about to accomplish this annual ritual according to our pact. Here is the warm heart of one of God's creatures. "

Suddenly, the fallen angel himself appeared. He was dressed in red, with a black cloak on top. Lucifer smiled broadly, took the heart from Bzinkem, sucked some blood from it, bit off a piece, and chewed with relish. He handed back the heart to Bzinkem.

"That tastes good," he said. "Now, eat it, my son. You have fulfilled your yearly ritual sacrifice to me. Thanks to you I have succeeded in influencing one more evil act. You have done well my son and your reward shall be great. "

Satan patted Bzinkem on the back lovingly.

"You see, son, God is still very powerful; and, despite all my efforts on earth, he has remained unconquerable. I need to work harder to achieve my ultimate goal of bringing him down. , and only loyal and dedicated servants like you can enable me to fill the world with so much evil that good will have no place in it. When there is no good, there is no God. "

"We are ready to do whatever you say, master," Bzinkem said. "The world is full of greedy people like me. Where there is greed, evil easily prevails. "

"That is true," Satan said. "With evil all over the place, God will have no foothold on earth. That is why I want to spill as much blood as possible and actually cover the earth with dirty blood. It is just that my attempts are being constantly thwarted by the clean pure blood of this man Jesus. Just a drop of his blood has several times more power than a pool of my dirty blood. You see that I have to spill more and more if I am to succeed. I have encouraged ritual sacrifices all over the earth and these involve a lot of dirty blood, but I still need a lot more. "

"We are there for you," Bzinkem said. "After all, we enjoy a lot behind you."

"Now eat," Satan said. "And enjoy your meal."

Satan disappeared as suddenly as he had appeared, leaving Bzinkem to continue with his ritual sacrifice. The look on Bzinkem's face was sinister.

This was not the Bzinkem that was known in society. If any of Bzinkem's acquaintances had seen him at that time, they would have sworn that they had seen the devil himself.

Bzinkem went ahead with his gory meal and ate every piece of the heart. It took some time, but he ate with lots of appetite. Bzinkem went to the toilet, eased himself, and came back to the messy room. The mess was indescribable. There was blood clotted all over. The bed sheets, mattress and pillows were all reddened by the blood. The appearance of the room gave the impression of a slaughter house or a sacrificial room. Even Ngangdi's suit case had not been spared by the blood. The frightful knife and syringe were lying on the bed. There was however, no cause for concern. Satan always sent the Turunduchiha Demon to clean up. He worked like a hyena and survived on the blood. He did not spare even the slightest trace. By morning, the room would look as if no drop of blood had been spilled in it. Satan was also aware of the mess that could be left in the kitchen and the living room, so the Turunduchiha Demon's activities extended to anything that had been displaced during the sacrificial night.

Bzinkem was now satisfied. He had fulfilled his pact with Lucifer for the year and would now maintain his wealth, bring back his age by one year, and stay healthy. Bzinkem was actually about five hundred years old, but he had maintained the appearance of a sixty year old man. During his five hundred years of existence, he always lived as a top member of the society in whatever civilization he was living in; and, having been quite selective, he had lived in areas with comparatively high standards and affluence. He had lived in Alexandria, Marrakesh, Malindi, and the capital city of the *Monomatapa*. He was a much respected citizen in Cape Town long before the apartheid system. He had been a close friend of one of the greatest *Asantehene* in Ghana and had shared meals with some of the greatest *Kabaka*s in Uganda. He achieved this through this yearly gory ritual where he had to devour the heart of a young person. He stayed in one town for about ten years, and then moved to another so that his secret would not be discovered. When he moved out, he left no trace as to his next destination. Wherever he moved, he became a respectable and admirable person. He had only

14

three more years to be in the current town and had just done his seventh ritual sacrifice there.

The next day, he stayed at home all day. The day watchmen who had opened the gate and let him in when he had come with Ngangdi, was back on duty but he would never know that the stranger of yesterday had never left the house.

The servants would remain oblivious of the presence of a stranger in the house the previous night and the satanic sacrifice that had occurred during the night, for there were no suspicious traces of blood in the room where Ngangdi had been sacrificed or anywhere else in the house. There were no dirty dishes, cutlery, or cups to show that any person apart from Bzinkem had been in the house. Bzinkem was always very meticulous after each ritual killing and left nothing suspicious lying around. The Turunduchiha Demon, for its part, was very thorough, even in the kitchen. Everything that had been used in the night was back where the servants had left it the previous day.

Life in Bzinkem's house went on as usual. He continued his life of a good citizen, fervent Christian, and gentleman. On the other hand, nobody would notice that he was not quite aging.

Bzinkem never went visiting anybody. Out of his house, he went to church or to his club. He shared a drink in a public place or attended meetings to which he was invited. He was now feeling quite okay and happy after his successful fulfilment of his pact with Satan for the year.

2

The fiends had a world leader just like the Catholics have a Pope and the Greek and Russian Orthodox churches have a Patriarch. This super-fiend was generally known as the Grand Baron and lived in Megido, the headquarters of fiend worship on earth. His abode was a large castle with a large courtyard for satanic feasts. There were many rooms in the castle, always prepared to receive high evil guests that often stopped by to consult with the Grand Baron. The current Grand Baron was Kadabra, a veteran fiend who had existed for about three thousand years. His two closest aides were Abra and Alakazam, and together with them, the Grand Baron had committed as much evil on earth as could fill the Pacific Ocean.

The Grand Baron had roving ambassadors that he often sent to represent him or to go round and reinforce the evil machinery and traps set up all over the world. After these ambassadors, the next in the hierarchy were the Grand Fiends. The Grand Fiend was the most senior fiend in each continent and each Grand Fiend started office with a pilgrimage to Megido where the final confirmation ceremony took place. The Grand Fiends in each continent reported directly to the Grand Baron.

Having lived for about three thousand years, Grand Baron Kadabra had become quite presumptuous. He had committed grievous crimes against humanity, propagated as much evil as possible, and had gone unscathed. The human God could claim that he was greater than Satan but he was virtually a toothless bulldog. He was too slow to anger, too forgiving, and too tolerant. That was how Satan had been

17

gaining the upper hand and how he had succeeded in protecting the Grand Baron in all his hideous crimes against God's people.

Satan had actually been one of God's closest angels and God had loved him like a son. Even after Satan's revolt, God's love for him still lingered, and this made God to hesitate to crush Satan mercilessly. God even allowed him once in a while to take certain liberties, which pained the archangels to no extent. As usual, Satan had seized this opportunity and even tried to temp God's own son at one time.

Despite his complacent and forgiving nature, there were occasions when God was stretched to the limits of his tolerance. On such occasions, God reacted with destructive anger and severely punished whomever had allowed himself to be misled by Satan. Having realized that it was not easy to challenge and defeat God in a fair battle, Satan had thus resorted to such methods of attracting God's anger on his own people. In the days of Noah, Satan worked very hard and planted evil all over the world, even in animals. God's anger was thus so great that it touched the whole world. Apart from Noah and his family, everybody else died in the flood that God sent. The Bible gives vivid details of what happened in Sodom and Gomorrah: God again showed that, when extremely provoked, he could react with packed violence. In some cases, however, he still hesitated to destroy human life. In the case of the construction of the tower of Babel, he actually avoided striking the people themselves, simply creating language confusion so that construction work would be frustrated.

The activities of Grand Baron Kadabra had already provoked God to an extreme and beyond. Baron Kadabra had actually trained Count Dracula and assisted him in developing a serious following of vampires. The Grand Baron had created sects of witches and wizards all over the world, and had even succeeded in getting a strong man in Haiti to take advantage to the suffering of black slaves to develop evil Zombies out of dead men. He had created terrible leaders like Ivan the Terrible, Red Erik, Attila the Hun, and many others. He had provoked the chaos in the Middle East where thousands of Christian crusaders and thousands of local tribesmen had perished. He had introduced and disseminated satanic beliefs and religions that placed human sacrifice and other ungodly practices at the centre of their rituals. Grand Baron Kadabra would stop at nothing to eliminate any good on earth. More recently, he had introduced hard drugs and, not satisfied with that, provoked all the violence that went along with it.

The word antichrist had actually originated from the Grand Baron. He had helped Satan to push the world into such violence, evil, and sin that God was obliged to send his only son to come and redeem the world. The Grand Baron had been the tool that Satan used to make Christ's birth difficult and to work for his early death. After his death and resurrection, however, the Grand Baron had discovered that Christianity was catching on rapidly; he had not succeeded in his mission. He had gone back to the drawing board and developed the movement of the antichrists.

Although this movement had worked hard - through vampires, zombies, witches, wizards and evil priests,–and initiated gory rituals, the followers of Christ had kept growing strong. , Eventually, the Grand Baron had developed the strategy of penetrating these followers of Christ and passing through some of them to achieve his malicious aims. He had used demented pastors like Jim Jones; these men ended up sacrificing their followers to the devil. He had created sects where honest Christians became members, only to end up realizing that they were serving the devil. Evil societies had grown, using the name of Christ and the Cross to propagate their evil activities. But still, God had remained strong and unconquerable, and tolerant.

The Grand Baron was now developing another great strategy to please his master Satan and help him conquer the world. He was going to use irresistible women to penetrate all the Christian leaders, starting from the Pope, the Patriarchs, the Anglican Arch Bishops, the Great Baptist, Presbyterian leaders, the Cardinals, Arch Bishops, Bishops, and priests. These females had been recruited from all over the world and were being indoctrinated in Megido. They were also being loaded with demonic powers that would make them irresistible, convincing, and very poisonous. The idea was that they would go back to the different parts of the world from which they had been recruited, lure these church leaders into sex, and transform them into servants of Lucifer. Training, indoctrination, and the provision of demonic powers had been going on for six months, and the women were now ready to be sent out on their destructive mission. Lucifer was getting closer to success, thanks to the relentless efforts of the Grand Baron. Given the homosexual tendencies of some church leaders, some young men had been included.

Their graduation ceremony was indeed great. The girls were all gathered in the courtyard of the Grand Baron's castle, about ten thousand of them, each strikingly beautiful and bent on wreaking havoc on pastors and priests. As the Grand Baron came out to dedicate them to his evil purpose and dispatch them to all the corners of the world, Lucifer himself appeared from nowhere and stood smiling, appreciating the gathering of radiant females. The Grand Baron smiled at him and continued with his ceremony.

Suddenly there was a loud trumpet sound and Angel Michael appeared in the sky in a golden chariot. As suddenly as he had appeared, Satan disappeared into the ground, leaving the now unprotected Baron Kadabra to face the wrath of God alone. It was not long in coming. Angel Michael unleashed a thunderbolt that struck the Grand Baron directly in the heart and his body burst into flames. In less than a minute he had been transformed into a mere heap of ash. The Angel hurled another big ball of fire which, circulating among the throng of beauties, simply cleaned them of the demonic powers that had been instilled into them. The other servants of Satan who had been assisting the Grand Baron scattered in different directions, but they all ended up as heaps of ash as Angel Michael hurled thunderbolts in their various directions. Satisfied with his work, Angel Michael finally turned his chariot around and disappeared into the sky.

The Grand Baron was dead after three thousand years of evil. For Satan's Kingdom to continue, he had to be replaced immediately. This called for a world reunion of senior fiends to elect, from among the Grand Fiends, the successor of the Grand Baron.

Bzinkem booked his flight and made sure that his passport was complete with the necessary visas. He had informed everybody that he was taking a trip to Switzerland to visit a friend with whom he had worked in the diplomatic field. He was actually heading for Megido to participate in the choosing of a new Grand Baron. Only Grand Fiends were eligible for election as Grand Baron but Bzinkem was a Senior Fiend, and all Senior Fiends formed part of the electorate and delegates to the election conference. Megido was supposed to be somewhere in the Middle East. This great distance placed it out of flying range for a fiend owl. When it came to travelling across oceans, seas, and continents, the fiends travelled like normal passengers on aircrafts.

On the departure day, Bzinkem's driver drove him to the airport and waited for the plane to leave. As usual, Bzinkem had left him with a heavy tip and the driver was straining on the leash to share his good fortune with his colleagues and friends. That evening the boozing was going to be hectic.

There was no direct flight to Jerusalem so Bzinkem had a stopover in Paris before getting there. He looked for a hotel with doors that opened onto balconies that could serve as take-off pads in the night. He was sure many other fiends had arrived and were looking for such strategic bases.

The Receptionist smiled beautifully as she filled in information about Bzinkem and advised him on which rooms opened to balconies on the other side of the hotel, away from the main street. In his room, Bzinkem had a bath, poured himself a cognac from the drinks in the cupboard, and sat waiting. He switched on the TV. After a while, he snoozed off. Three hours later, he got up from sleep. It was thirty minutes past eight, and it was quite dark already. He still had about one and a half hours to wait. His flight to Megido would take about thirty minutes, and it was always advisable to take off and fly after ten p. m. when there was no longer any danger of being spotted.

By ten o'clock in the night, he was fully dressed for the conference. He opened the door to the balcony and went out.

After surveying to make sure that no body was watching, he took off as an owl and headed towards Megido.

There was much bustle in Megido as senior fiends kept arriving. Megido was not quite like modern cities of today. The streets were all cobbled and the houses looked like toadstools growing in some organized order. The greyish castle of the Grand Fiend stood in the middle of the city and towered high above the array of toadstools. There were no vehicles in Megido as the inhabitants simply floated or flew to their destinations. There was animal life available. There were ponds full of piranha, and the sky was regularly rent by harsh eerie croaks and shrieks from strange looking vultures and crows. Vampire bats hung from lamp posts and the available oak trees. There were pets, too. While some inhabitants kept wolves, hyenas, and ebony black or pure white cats, others preferred cobras and mambas as pets. There were sports grounds in Megido where they used human heads as balls and human bones as bats. Human hair was the material used for making their nets. There were bars and night clubs too, where blood was served as drink and the musicians played on drums made of human skin and bones. Dancing in these night clubs was virtually like what takes place in normal cities on earth but for the fact that the dancers kind of floated in the air slightly above the floor. The music itself was like the wailing of a lost soul when it was slow, or like the shrieks and growls of tigers fighting when it was fast. Megido was really a city of its own, and the inhabitants did not need to earn an income in order to survive.

The Grand Fiends were all dressed in wine coloured cloaks and bowties, and completely white suits and shoes. Each of them was hopeful and already dreaming of becoming the greatest fiend on earth. Choosing a Grand Baron, just like choosing the Grand Fiends, was interesting to watch. It looked like fair elections but was always fraught with high rigging, hitting below the belt, and every kind of election fraud imaginable. The irony of it all was that, after all the struggle, Lucifer always jumped in and declared his own winner. Of course, there can never be any democracy in hell.

While the senior fiends were gathering for this bizarre election process, Succubus, Jezebel, and other female fiends of a certain rank were organizing for the feast that would take place at the end. There were Russian female fiends led by the svelte Nagaina, beautiful Inca women led by Rascala Huapac, cute Aztecs led by Popocatepli, and lots of very attractive females. A tall, very blond Scandinavian known as Ingridfiendsen and a smallish Chukchi fiend were quite popular. There were many others from all over the world to take care of the lusts of the senior fiends during the sexual orgies that always accompanied such occasions. The senior fiends could have their pick of graceful Kenyan and South African girls, stout Quicha females, short, roundish Mongol and Eskimo females, seductive Arab and Indian girls, sexy Russian girls, you name them. This wide choice of sexual partners did not exclude beautiful lady boys from Bangkok, she-males from Brazil and other transsexuals recruited from around France and Italy.

Feeding was well organized; and liver, kidneys, lungs, intestines, genitals, hearts, and blood were available in abundance. The source of all these could be traced to a few sudden disasters that occurred in parts of the world. On the eve of the occasion, a pleasure boat had suddenly crashed on some rocks in the Mediterranean, and the passengers had provided body parts for the feast. A tsunami that suddenly struck somewhere along an Asian coast provided more body parts. This was completed with body parts from an eruption somewhere in Latin America. Everything was transported fresh by the servant demons to Megido.

The Election process started and as each candidate and his followers tried to rig it, a free for all started. As usual. Demonic fighting is generally more violent than human skirmishes. The brawl was even more confusing given the fact that there were no specific sides pitted against each other. Blows, scratches and bites were destined for any fiend who happened not to be in your camp. Suddenly, there were loud claps of thunder and Lucifer appeared.

"These are true sons of Lucifer," he said, "full of violence, treachery, dirty tricks, and evil. You have proven your worth and I am proud of all of you. "

All the senior fiends went down on their knees to honour Satan.

```````"Now," Satan said, "we have all democratically elected the Aztec senior fiend Itzcoliuhqui, who is now the Grand Fiend of North America, as the Grand Baron. "

"Praise be to the great Lucifer," the senior fiends chorused.

"We are through with that; and the Grand Baron Itzcoliuhqui, is now installed," Satan said conclusively.

The Grand Baron Itzcoliuhqui stepped out from the crowd and went up to Satan who bit off a small chunk of flesh from his chest and swallowed. Itzcoliuhqui then led Satan to the alter where hearts and genitals of the victims that had been killed to supply food for the occasion had been heaped. This was where Satan was going to be entertained alongside the Grand Fiends. Every other fiend was to move to the tables lined up on the other side of the courtyard and
```````

occupy himself with whatever he chose. Available were liver, lungs, spleens, and intestines.

But before this, Satan had to conduct a small ritual with the new Grand Baron. He pointed at one of sexual organs lying in a tray.

"I will have that one," he said.

It was a huge penis attached to a very heavy and massive sack that contained two large testicles. Satan picked it up and started chewing.

"I will have Tibetan blood for a drink this time," he said. "And where is that whore Succubus? Succubus will keep me company for the feast. "

He picked up a heart from the tray in front of him and continued eating. Satan really had a ravenous appetite. As Succubus joined him, the Grand Fiends also made their choice of female fiends for the orgy. The other female fiends mingled among the senior fiends. Bzinkem took for himself a beautiful Filipino girl, while his two table mates opted for some beautiful Thai lady-boys. The feast was already in progress, full of gore and sex.

The feast lasted virtually throughout the night. The climax of it all was the dancing. This was a worldwide occasion and an occasion for fiends of the highest order. It would have been expected, therefore, that the dancing would be orderly and devoid of chaotic behaviour. But then, this was a gathering of fiends with Satan, who was bent on forgetting the disgrace he had recently received from Angel Michael. The dancing was full of erotic displays, scratching, scuffles, and sex. Only Satan could keep a female full-time to himself. The general tendency among the others was to seize a female from another fiend the moment they concluded that she was performing wonderfully and the fiend was enjoying himself thoroughly. They were like cocks who abandon a pretty hen just to go chase another cock away from an ugly hen. The noise itself ranged from sharp screeches to hideous snarls, hisses, and growls. The noise would have been ear-splitting and unbearable to humans; but, to these demons, it was a normal way of expressing excitement and enjoyment. Some of the noise expressed pain, such as when a fiend received a deep gash in the flesh, or disappointment, such as when a juicy female was snatched away by another fiend.

Bzinkem finally had the opportunity of snatching off from another fiend, an Ethiopian belle that he had been eying all along. He turned her round and they immediately went into action. Just then he noticed a Burmese fiend next to him apparently coming close to an orgasm as he straddled a plump Bedouin female. He immediately abandoned the Ethiopian, booted off the Burmese fiend, and replaced him. He had just three minutes of the Bedouin as one of the descendants of Attila picked him up from the woman and threw him into a crowd of revellers. Bzinkem simply turned round and deprived a Turk of a Tasmanian blond with long sharp nails.

The feasting area was red with gore, an indication that the Turunduchiha demon would have a lot of work to do early the following morning.

By six a. m. Bzinkem was already snoring in his hotel room. His soiled clothes in which he had flown back, were bundled in a black plastic bag, which he would dispose of in any thrash can. He had cleaned himself thoroughly when he came back into his room through the balcony door, and now looked like an honest hotel guest that had been sleeping blissfully throughout the night.

Bzinkem got up around 12 noon, had another thorough bath to ensure that there was no speck of blood on him, and went to the Jerusalem airport to take a homeward-bound plane. They had now installed a Grand Baron to every fiend's satisfaction.

3

Three months later, Bzinkem was on his way to attend a meeting. As the driver swerved to avoid hitting another vehicle, Bzinkem suddenly felt the familiar pain in his groin. He had to do something about it fast or he might end up losing one of his greatest pleasures in life.

"Take me to my club," he told the driver

"You will no longer attend the meeting, sir?" the driver asked.

Bzinkem had been on his way to a fundraising meeting for the construction of a public library.

"No," Bzinkem answered. "I just remembered that I had an appointment. "

The driver drove to the club and parked in one of the parking lots.

"Eh, Anchang," Bzinkem said as he was coming out of the car.

"Sir?" the driver replied.

"Give me the keys of the car. I will drive myself home," Bzinkem said. "And Anchang?"

"Yes, sir?" the driver answered.

"I will have supper here before I go back home. Tell the others that they can go home as well," Bzinkem said, handing over three crisp banknotes to Anchang.

As Anchang left, Bzinkem went into the club and asked for a cognac. He needed a stiff drink

His task this time was a bit more difficult, and it was a task that had to be performed every five years. The pain in the groin had indicated that it was time. The yearly ritual to extend his lifespan and keep him slightly above middle age involved one man. The present ritual required two persons, a man and a woman. It was easier to lure a man into his house and sacrifice him. It was not the same when you had to convince a strange couple to spend the night in your house. Well, he had done it many times before, but each time he had to apply a lot of tact. As the cognac burned his insides, he eyed a young couple that seemed to be enjoying each other's company thoroughly. Those would have been perfect victims only that they would be missed if they disappeared and it could be traced to him. He needed perfect strangers to the town and a big motor park. A simple bus station would not do.

He came out of the club and drove to the busiest motor park where he spent the whole afternoon looking out for a suitable couple. He actually found some but dismissed them because they were accompanied by children. Two couples that had no children turned out to be siblings. Two other couples had just returned from visiting relatives and were heading straight back to their homes. By nightfall his search had not yielded any victims so he drove home, got high on cognac, and slept soundly.

The next day after breakfast, he gave everybody a holiday and drove to another busy motor park. He was now dressed like any ordinary man, not the usual aristocratic outfit. He parked carefully and made sure the car was locked. You could never be too sure in rowdy areas like motor parks. They always abounded with pick pockets and persons who were watching out for any opportunity to grab and make away with what was not theirs. He moved to one of the numerous beer joints and opted for a seat from which he could observe most alighting passengers from the various buses.

The drinking joint was strategically located although it could not be considered as comfortable. There were poorly made wooden benches with bare wooden tables on which you could stand your beer. There were no drinking glasses and every customer sipped directly from the bottle. Assorted beer and sweet drinks were sold alongside a few snacks, like fried chicken, goat meat, and snails. Hawkers moved in and out advertising their wares and urging everybody to buy. Next door, a woman was selling cooked food. On a table in front of her, she had several food flasks from which she served the food. Her customers sat on wooden benches, where they ate food in plastic plates and drank water from plastic cups

Bzinkem had asked for a bottle of Guinness, the only drink among the range of local beers that his delicate palate could accommodate. He was now sipping slowly and watching attentively as passengers were coming down from a bus that had just arrived. There were quite a number of passengers, but no convincing couple.

The next bus soon arrived and was subjected to the close scrutiny of Bzinkem. He sighed after he realized that all the passengers had come out of the bus and were dispersing. His efforts were bearing no fruits. Two other buses arrived but with disappointing results. Bzinkem looked at his gold omega watch and noticed that it was already three 0'clock in the afternoon. He had been sitting there for three hours and the bar man was probably unhappy that he was occupying space without consuming. He called for another bottle of Guinness and, since he was feeling rather hungry, he decided to accompany it with a piece of goat meat. He was chewing carefully, cautious not to drop anything on his shirt, when he noticed something promising. A young man in his thirties by Bzinkem's assessment had just come out of a bus and was helping a woman to alight. When she came down, she gave him a peck on the jaw and said something to the man, looking fondly at him. Bzinkem could not hear what she was saying to the man because of the distance, but he was sure there was some genuine intimacy between the couple. Bzinkem took a swig of stout and concentrated on the couple. They were now holding hands, waiting for their luggage to be sent down from the carriage.

Bzinkem watched closely. Maybe he was lucky this time. He stood up slowly and waited for the couple to retrieve their luggage and start moving away. He did not have to wait long as their luggage was quickly lowered to them. This was the time. He came out of the drinking joint, abandoning the rest of his drink and goat meat, and started moving towards them as they moved away from the bus. Everything was working as he wanted.

Suddenly something went wrong. Some blasted fellow shouted from one angle of the motor park where private vehicles were parked. He had been leaning against a blue Peugeot parked close to Bzinkem's vehicle and probably waiting for this specific couple that Bzinkem was targeting. The couple swung around in the direction of the voice, noticed the man, waved at him, and started moving towards him. Bzinkem stopped in his tracks, pretended to have forgotten something, and retreated to the booze joint where he had been sitting. The bar man had already cleared off his drink and meat, but his strategic vantage point was still available. He sat down and called for another bottle of Guinness, but this time opted for a piece of chicken. The goat meat was rather tough.

Bzinkem sat for another thirty minutes and nodded off. He would have missed a wonderful opportunity if the attentive bar man had not noticed that he had snoozed off and come to wake him up. The bar man was used to the fact that persons often came to pick up incoming visitors and ended up waiting for almost the whole day.

"Waiting for somebody, sir?" he asked.

Bzinkem was immediately awakened by the voice. He was supposed to be watching not sleeping.

"Thank you," he told the bar man" They are sending my little niece to me unaccompanied, so I have to wait for her and pick her up. "

"Then you have to remain attentive, sir. " the bar man said. "A bus has just arrived and she may be on it. "

"I am very grateful for that," Bzinkem said. "Please, have two beers on me. "

"Thank you very much, sir. " the barman said. "I spend the whole day in this bar watching others drink but with no possibility of quenching my own thirst. My meagre salary does not allow for that. It is only when a generous person like you comes along that I can have access to a drink. "

As the bar man moved away to serve another client, Bzinkem continued watching. He noticed a man who had come out from the bus standing and waiting for his luggage. It did not mean anything to him as he was interested but in couples. Suddenly he saw one of the female passengers, who had come out of the bus among the last, move up to the man. She was apparently complaining about something. Bzinkem noticed the man explode angrily but could not understand what was transpiring as he was far off in the drinking spot. However, he observed even more closely, trying to make out what was transpiring. He noticed the man move up to some official of the bus service, talking and gesticulating wildly. Maybe he could get closer and find out what was happening.

Bzinkem stood up and moved towards the bus. The young woman he had noticed was talking desperately to another passenger so Bzinkem moved up to her.

"What should be the matter, madam?" he asked.

"Are you an official here?" she asked.

"Not really," Bzinkem answered. "But I may be in a position to help if I only knew what the problem was. "

"We have been robbed," she said with lots of despair. "All our money was in my handbag and some thieve sneaked it away. "

"How?" Bzinkem asked. "A woman is always attached to her handbag. "

"I fell asleep towards the end of the journey and only got up when we had arrived and passengers were moving out. This thief had carefully opened my handbag, rummaged inside and extracted the money. Unfortunately for me, it was all in an envelope so his task was easy. "

"Your husband did not notice the thief at work?" asked Bzinkem "He must have been sitting by you. "

This was a shot in the dark. The answer to this question would tell Bzinkem whether the angry man was her husband or not. He was lucky.

"My husband was sitting two seats away in front," she replied. "We booked late for this bus and could not find two free seats that were next to each other. "

Bzinkem was quite satisfied.

"Is that your husband ranting over there" he asked.

"He is," she replied. "He has a right to be angry. Bus services should not allow pick-pockets to operate freely in their buses. What shall we do now? We are visitors to this town and all our money is gone. "

Bzinkem smiled inwardly. This would be a wonderful catch.

"Call for your husband," he said to her. "All that ranting will take you nowhere. Rather, I can help you. "

"Dear," she shouted to her husband. "This gentleman here wants to speak to you. He thinks he can help. "

"What can he do? With all our money gone, we are lost," the man replied in frustration.

"Just come and let us hear what he has to say," the woman replied.

The man came across looking very disappointed with everything.

"Let us seat somewhere and talk," Bzinkem said. "My car is parked over there so maybe we could discuss inside. "

After they retrieved their luggage, he led them to the car and they all settled inside.

"Now tell me what the problem is," Bzinkem said.

"Thank you for trying to be of help to us," the man said, "but may we know who you are first? My name is Nchoji and this is my wife Manitia. "

"I am called Muluo," Bzinkem lied, "and I am one of the top lawyers in town. "

It was necessary to keep his name secret and, since he had no specific profession, he had to invent one. In society, he was simply known as a retired senior diplomat.

"My wife and I are lucky to have met you," the man said.

"Feel free with me," Bzinkem said. "I am sure I can help you. "

"Well," said Nchoji, "we actually live in Muloin, a small town to the North West of the country. Manitia's brother, who has been out of the country for fifteen years, is coming back home so we travelled down to receive him. "

"When is he coming?" Bzinkem asked.

"His plane lands tomorrow night," Manitia said. "We travelled here today so as not to be caught up by any unforeseen circumstances, but now we are in a jam. "

"So you were coming to spend the night here and receive him tomorrow?" Bzinkem asked.

"Quite so," Nchoji said.

"And did you have any particular place in mind where you thought you would sleep?" asked the cunning Bzinkem. "A friend, maybe, or a relative?"

"Not really," said Nchoji. "We were coming to sleep in a hotel and then hire a taxi tomorrow night and pick up her brother at the airport. "

"And now you have lost all your money," Bzinkem said.

"Unfortunately so," Nchoji said. "We are total strangers to you but the biggest help you could give us would be a loan. I promise you, we will pay it back when Manitia's brother comes. If it happens that he does not have enough money, we shall send it to you when we go back to Muloin. We have some of these money transfer agencies out there. "

"I can't simply trust you like that with my money," Bzinkem said. "But you look like honest people so I could play host to you today and take you in my car to the airport tomorrow to receive madam's brother. "

"We don't want to put you to so much trouble," Nchoji said. "All we need is a little money to permit us sleep in the cheapest hotel and enable us get to the airport tomorrow. "

"It would rather be a pleasure for me to host you in my house. There are many comfortable rooms which will cost you nothing. Tomorrow my car will be at your disposal; but, if you insist, I will give you money for a taxi then. "

Nchoji looked at his wife. They were both helpless, and this stranger was offering a way out. He had an expensive car and most probably a comfortable house. They could at least spend the night and borrow enough the next day to continue on their own.

"What do you say Manitia?" he asked his wife.

"I think this gentleman is God sent," Manitia said. "Let's accept his hospitality. "

Nchoji and Manitia could never have imagined that such a soft-spoken, smooth talker was actually a servant of Satan.

"I would have insisted that you accept my hospitality any way," Bzinkem said. "When I saw your husband at the motor park, something struck me, before I realised that there was some trouble and stepped in. "

"What was it that struck you concerning my husband?" Manitia asked.

"Let's go to the house and you will see. " Bzinkem said.

Bzinkem drove through jammed streets to his house. It was already rush hour and drivers cursed as other drivers drove poorly, or as motorcycle taxis meandered recklessly in the heavy traffic. Bzinkem was a good driver and a calm one at that. He never got himself into the habit of cursing, not even when highly provoked. Drivers in the wrong always wait for the slightest opportunity to lash back, and they always get disappointed when the wronged driver ignores them.

They finally got to Bzinkem's house and the gate was opened by a night watchman. It was already getting dark. Nchoji was quite impressed, even scared as he saw the magnificent villa. Their host was certainly of the highest class and a very rich man. But what was such a rich man looking for in a motor park, a service used mainly by the poor and average class?

They came out of the car and Bzinkem led them in. The living room was quite specious with several sets of very expensive chairs. Bzinkem took them to one corner where a large portrait picture apparently of Nchoji was hanging.

"Madam," he said, "here is your answer to my reason for being interested in your husband when I saw him at the bus station and the reason why I deciding to help. I was struck by the resemblance between your husband and my son. "

"Your son?" Manitia asked confused. "The face in that picture looks exactly like my husband. "

"That was my only son," Bzinkem said, looking sadly at the picture. "His mother died five years earlier of leukaemia. He crashed his own car last year, killing himself, his wife, and their two sons. "

"How sad," Manitia said compassionately

"You see, despite all this wealth, I am a lonely old man. "

"It must have been very difficult and hard on you to lose an only son," Nchoji said.

"You can imagine the emotion inside me when I saw you at the motor park. It was just as if my son had come back. "

"But what was such a man like you doing out there at the motor park?" Nchoji asked.

"I want to start a bus service, a very big one. My experts have carried out all the studies but, you know, we businessmen who have some flair always want to put in a personal touch. For three days now, I have driven there each day and observed things myself in order to pick up certain hints. I was lucky I went there today or I would never have met somebody who looks so much like my son. "

"Rather," said Manitia, "we were lucky that you came or we would have been completely stranded. "

"Let's forget about my biological son for now," Bzinkem said. "I have met a replacement. Let's move over there and sit down. "

As they sat down, Nchoji was admiring everything around. Everything in the living room looked quite expensive and was just in the right place.

"I am sure you are famished," Bzinkem said. "Manitia could go to the kitchen and arrange something. "

"You don't have servants?" Nchoji asked in surprise.

"I do," replied Bzinkem, "but they have all closed. I normally don't want to overwork them. In the evenings, I can serve myself a snack or a drink so I don't have to oblige them to stay late. "

Bzinkem picked up the remote control and switched on the TV then turned to Nchoji

"There are assorted drinks in the cupboard over there and beers in the kitchen. Serve yourself. "

Shortly after, Manitia emerged from the kitchen. She had found food already prepared and simply had to warm it up and bring it out. She placed the food on the dining table and invited everybody to it.

"I hope you and your wife drink wine," Bzinkem said. "There is very good wine. "

"We do," Manitia said.

"Good," Bzinkem said and went to a different cupboard where he brought out the wine. It was special wine laced with some powerful aphrodisiac. He gave the bottle to Nchoji and showed him where the wine opener and wine glasses were found. Nchoji opened the wine and poured for everybody. As Bzinkem sipped from his glass, he watched with satisfaction as Nchoji and Manitia drank from theirs. Those two were bound to make hectic love that night. The aphrodisiac was strong and very effective.

After the meal, Manitia was about to clear the table but Bzinkem stopped her.

"Don't worry about all that," Bzinkem said. "You are my honourable guests. The servants will take care of that. Just make yourselves comfortable and enjoy your drink. I can see there is still some wine left in the bottle, or would you prefer something else?"

"Thank you, Mr Muluo," she replied. "I think I will continue with the wine. It tastes quite good. "

"You could call me Dad," Bzinkem said. "Your husband is just like my son now. The resemblance is so great that I would do anything for you. This relationship must continue. You must promise me that you will be coming once in a while to stay with me. "

"That is no problem at all," Nchoji said. "You are a wonderful host. "

"Tomorrow we shall exchange phone numbers," Bzinkem said. "That way, we shall keep constantly in touch. "

They were now comfortably ensconced in the comfortable seats in front of one of the large TV screens.

"You must be a very successful business man," Nchoji said, still admiring everything around him.

"But I thought he said he is a lawyer. " Manitia said.

"That is true," Bzinkem said. "And a very successful one. But, as you see today, when you have much money, you strive to have even more. That is why I got into business. "

While watching TV, they conversed on various topics until Nchoji who had become quite horny from the aphrodisiac in the wine decided that it was late enough for sleep.

"I think we should retire now," he said. "We have had a long tiring journey and need quite some rest. "

Bzinkem thought it was still a bit early for his night's sacrifice. He needed at least an hour more.

"It is just eight o'clock," he said, "and tomorrow you don't have to get up early. I hardly ever have good company like this, so please keep me company until at least nine o'clock. "

Manitia though equally desirous of the attention of her husband, thought they should please this generous host. One extra hour of waiting was not that much.

"No problem, Dad," she said in a placating manner. "We shall stay with you even till morning. "

They all laughed at this.

"That will not be necessary," Bzinkem said. "Your room is the second to the right if you follow that corridor. It should be quite comfortable. "

"Thank you very much, Dad," Manitia said.

Finally it was Bzinkem who decided it was time to retire. By his watch, it was thirty minutes past nine.

"I have kept you up long enough," he said, "and I also need sleep. I wish you goodnight and will see you tomorrow at breakfast. "

"Goodnight," Nchoji and Manitia chorused.

As Nchoji and Manitia went into their room and locked the door, they had no time for preliminaries before sleep like brushing teeth and so on. They were already over worked by the Aphrodisiac. They immediately sprang into each other's arms and very soon were completely taken up by intensive

41

love making. So involved were they that they were oblivious to anything else. They would never know Bzinkem was watching them from a neighbouring room through a small window in the wall.

Bzinkem himself was fully excited as he had partaken of the drink laced with the aphrodisiac. As he watched the couple performing, he was rubbing his erect manhood and timing the climax. He was actually masturbating. As the couple came to a climax he also worked himself up to the apex and came along with them. This was the first step of the ritual. Bzinkem had taken over Nchoji's virility which would last for another five years. If Nchoji continued to live, he would be completely impotent.

The next step now was to get full confirmation from his master. He watched as the couple was lying exhausted in each other's arms and smiled sadistically. They had just had their last excitement. Bzinkem reached a secret switch and switched off the light in the room. Nchoji and his wife concluded that it was some black out. Anyway, they were too satisfied in each other's arms to bother.

Bzinkem opened a secret door and slipped into the room. His special shoes and practiced steps enabled him to move without the slightest noise. He was carrying two syringes loaded with some paralyzing liquid. It was always more exciting when the victim was aware that he was being sacrificed, without being capable of reacting. His task would be easy as both victims were lying naked. Any part of the body was alright for the injection to be applied. Bzinkem moved up stealthily to the bed and applied the needles at the places where he knew parts of their body would be.

Manitia felt a sharp pain on her buttocks and shrieked in pain. She had been lying on Nchoji's stomach. Just then

Nchoji too felt the same sharp pain as the needle penetrated deep into his thigh. He turned to find out what was happening and looked directly into the contorted face of Bzinkem. It was quite dark, but Bzinkem's face was glowing. Bzinkem switched on the lights and turned Manitia to also lie on her back. He moved Nchoji slightly to make room for Manitia's limp body. Nchoji and Manitia were now helpless as the powerful drug had already taken effect. On the other hand, they could see clearly what was happening. As they watched with horror, Bzinkem brought out an ugly, sharp knife from the long grey robe he was now wearing and proceeded to slice off Manitia's breasts which he dropped into a bowl. Then, he thrust the knife deep into Manitia's chest, just where the heart was, and watched her die. Nchoji was frantic but helpless.

Bzinkem now turned to Nchoji and smiled sardonically as he saw the fright on his face. He gathered Nchoji's penis and testicles and sliced them off with the ugly knife. As Nchoji lay helpless, not even capable of writhing in pain, Bzinkem trust the knife deep into his chest too, and watched him die.

The room was quite a mess now, soiled sheets and gore all over. Bzinkem picked up the breasts and held them together with Nchoji's genitals

"Oh, great master," he said. "Your servant has done it again. He is now offering to you this special feast so that you give him sexual prowess as usual and enable him to enjoy life the way your servants should. "

Satan appeared as before in his red attire and black cloak. His face was quite strange and it was difficult to determine whether he was green, blue, or grey. His smile was quite ugly and frightening.

"You have made me proud again," Satan said to Bzinkem. "Yes, I give my servants long life, wealth, sex, and lots of fun on earth. Is that not what you want?"

"We are very thankful, Great Master," said Bzinkem. "All your servants are greedy, self-centred, wicked, and glutinous. We want all the pleasures of the earth for ourselves and do not care how we get them. "

"That is why I say you are one of my best servants," Satan said. "Unfortunately, the majority of the people on earth are fools. They still believe in God. Now, tell me, what do they see in a God who gives them short lives on earth and prefers to call them early to heaven where they are bound to live very dull lives? I was once there you know, and life was quite dull. "

"It is certainly still quite dull," Bzinkem said. "I am sure of that master. "

"And apart from the dull life, God does not give them all the fun I give you. He restricts them from fornication, bans them from acquiring what they desire by stealth or by force, and warns them against killing those who annoy them. He tries to prevent them from taking what they want. "

"I wonder who would prefer such restrictions," Bzinkem said.

"Even the music and dances in heaven are quite boring and solemnly religious," Satan said. "On earth, most people prefer lively, sexy, or comic rhythms. In heaven, there is no Makossa, bottle dance or Soukous where women gyrate their buttocks obscenely and make men happy. And no rap music either with lots of swear words and obscenities. "

"Yes, master. All they do out there in heaven is sing praises to that pompous God. Ridiculous. "

"I still remember when I lived in that damn place called heaven before I was cast out," Satan said. "I managed to remain there for all that while simply because I had my plans to stage a take-over from God. "

"That would have been wonderful," Bzinkem said.

"I was close to taking over absolute power. If only this God's slave they call Michael had not succeeded in defeating me and my demons. Yes, that was a great battle. I took the form of a dragon and spewed fire all over but Michael still found a way out. Anyway, let them rot up there in heaven while I control the earth. Total control of the earth is now my dream and target. "

"Master, you have almost succeeded," Bzinkem said. "The earth is virtually yours already. Many of the supposed men of God act according to your dictates. They are fornicators, embezzlers, thieves, murderers; you name any evil on earth. "

"And there are women, too," Satan said. "My success could easily be guaranteed by women. "

"Women?" Bzinkem asked.

"Yes," Satan replied. "You can use a woman to do anything evil. Most men do criminal and evil things because they are either provoked or enticed by a woman. They kill each other for the love of a woman. They rob and kill to acquire enough wealth to satisfy the whims and caprices of a woman. They commit murder and savage acts because they are provoked by a woman's infidelity and lack of commitment. Many men develop the habit of taking drugs just because they need the Dutch courage that will enable them to chat up a woman. "

"You are right master," Bzinkem said. "The root cause of every evil or criminal act can always be linked to a woman. "

45

"Women have always been my accomplices since they are easy to capture. I seduced Adam's first wife, Lilith, and transformed her into a demon. Quite sweet, that one, and she became quite loyal. God went ahead and gave Adam another wife, Eve, and made sure that she was now subordinate to him. I still succeeded in using my charms on her, although I could no longer transform her into a demon. Still, I succeeded in using her to make Adam disobey God so that they would get thrown down to earth where I would have easy access to them," Satan said. "If Adam had remained in that garden, it would have been difficult for me to penetrate."

"That means, sending Adam out of that garden was a hasty decision on God's part?" Bzinkem asked.

"Sure. He made things easy for me," Satan said.

"On the other hand," said Bzinkem, "some of us, your servants, have difficult roles to play in order to effectively carry out our mission on earth. I am obliged to play the boring role of a good man and the revolting role of a fervent Christian in order to disguise my activities as a senior fiend. "

"Yes, as I told you before," Satan said, "having anything to do with God requires a lot of patience, commitment, and sacrifice. As for me, I offer people an easy life, without any tedious prayers and novenas. I offer them freedom to commit crimes, indulge in free sex, and do what they please. The small sacrifice you make through your pretence of being a good Christian is greatly rewarded by me. "

"I admit that," Bzinkem said.

"That sacrifice is simply a trap or a bait that you use in luring God's people into trusting you, and then striking like the fiend that you are. "

"We are trying our best to make you succeed," Bzinkem said.

"Yes, every sacrifice counts," Satan said. "And the more gruesome the better. "

Satan picked up one of the breasts. "I love these very much," he said. "Now you have to complete the beefing up of your manhood. Eat the genitals. "

Both of them started eating,

"I will send the Turunduchiha Demon to help clean up all this mess," Satan said. "Everything must be quite in order before your servants come in tomorrow. Now, give me one of those testicles. "

Bzinkem handed it over and continued wolfing up the rest of his ritual meat. Satan threw the testicle into his mouth and chewed with alacrity. He had already finished the two breasts which he had gulped down with ravenous appetite.

After the horrible meal, Satan disappeared and Bzinkem went to his room, cleaned himself up properly, and went to bed. The next day he would find the house in proper order, thanks to the mysterious Turunduchiha Demon. Nobody would even know that he had received guests the previous night.

As Bzinkem lay in bed, he smiled happily at the thought that he would be able to continue with his sexual escapades for the next five years with full vigour.

Bzinkem's regular three day trips each week to some unknown destination was not for nothing. The impression he gave in town that he was God-fearing and quite responsible when it came to relationships with females was far from reality. Actually, Bzinkem had a very active sexual life. He enjoyed sex, and the act constituted one of the main pillars of devil worship. Bzinkem's three days trips out of town were meant to fully indulge and exhaust all steam gathered during the other four days. Bzinkem spent those three days mostly locked up in an expensive hotel room with lots to eat and drink and as many sexy whores as his large appetite could accommodate. He had the money and could pay well for everything. He always made sure that he enjoyed himself thoroughly during these sex orgies.

4

During Sunday worship, Bzinkem always occupied one of the pews at the back of the church, far away from the altar and all the holiness and solemnity that goes with it. He was protected from any holy forces released from the altar by the floating sins and powers of the talismans of many of the members of the congregation who sat between him and the altar.

On this particular Sunday, he had an additional task. It was time to recruit another follower of Satan. All senior fiends had the duty of recruiting a follower of Satan each year, thus in each town through which Bzinkem passed, he recruited ten followers during his ten years stay. Recruiting such a servant was a delicate procedure; you had to be quite sure that the targeted person would accept before you made the final move. These followers of Satan would eventually graduate into fiends.

Bzinkem had already recruited six persons and was now targeting the seventh. The first one was a pastor, who turned out to be an easy catch. The next one was a female top journalist whose ambition to further her career was stronger than anything else. Next he had hooked a local parliamentarian who was bent on remaining in that position forever. Bzinkem had again turned to the female sex and recruited a business woman whose lust for wealth and power over men knew no bounds. Two more were later recruited, and now it was time for the seventh. These servants of Satan came in different forms and could be witches, wizards, or members of demonic secret cults. These persons cast spells, offered family members for ritual sacrifice, and hurled destructive curses around. Some of the wizards and witches participated in feasts where they transformed humans into animals and ate the flesh. Such future small time fiends achieved extended life spans only after they had died and resurfaced elsewhere, and it was on condition that they fulfilled all their basic obligations as servants of Satan during their normal lifespan.

In each continent, there was one Grand Fiend. In most prominent countries, there was a senior fiend and, in big cities, there were several small fiends and servants of Satan, specialized in some aspect of the occult or some kind of dark art. Small time witches and wizards were found in some prominent villages. At the lower levels, what adherents mostly strived for was to achieve power, position, wealth and influence. A few of them simply wanted to be irresistible to women. This was the kind of case Bzinkem had in hand now. He had been studying a fellow who always sat two pews in front of him during Sunday mass. In church, the man always prayed fervently and looked very pious. Outside, he ogled virtually every beautiful female he saw with obvious lust and dirty intensions. He was known to tickle the palms of females whenever he gave them a handshake and to seize every opportunity to hug them.

But, although he was rather good looking, he had been refused very often by females because of his lowly financial status. Bzinkem had, by chance, overheard some females commenting about the loose behaviour of the young man and his weakness for anything in skirt. He had made some enquires and discovered that the man indeed had a problem, and he had decided to get close to him. He had made it a point of inviting the man for a few drinks and a chat each

Sunday after church, and had learned much. The man was married and had three kids. He was a junior clerk in a government office and had been working for ten years. His salary was quite small and did not permit him to live the life he would have loved to live. He had admitted his weakness for women, but blamed God for making him like that.

Everything he said was quite interesting, but what impressed Bzinkem the most was the way his eyes kept roving over any female who happened to pass by. Even the ladies who served drinks or snacks seemed to stir his loins. Bzinkem finally came to the conclusion that he was on the right track and that this was his seventh candidate for recruitment. The man was aged about 40 years old and called Bemsi.

Bzinkem watched as Bemsi knelt fervently during offertory, closing his eyes and looking like one of God's angels. Lucifer probably looked like this when he was still a good boy and respected God. Many hard criminals, full of evil and wickedness, also revered God like this when they were still innocent kids.

Bzinkem had also noticed that Bemsi never failed to go up to donate alms but could not make out what he dropped in the alms box. Bemsi always went up for communion and walked back to his seat looking like he had never failed and would never fail God in his life. No one would have guessed that this hypocrite often imagined himself making love to the beautiful reverend sisters who often assisted the priest in giving communion.

As soon as mass ended, Bzinkem jumped out and waited for Bemsi. When Bemsi stepped out of church and saw Bzinkem beckoning, he moved over to meet him by his car.

"Bemsi," Bzinkem said, "I think we should meet after lunch and discuss something important. Say four o clocks?"

"No problem," Bemsi said. "I shan't be doing anything at that time and there is no serious football match programmed for today over T. V. "

"Ok, see you then," Bzinkem said.

"Where do we meet?" Bemsi asked

"I will pick you up at your house," Bzinkem said.

"You know where I live?" Bemsi asked in surprise.

"Of course," said Bzinkem. "You don't get close to somebody without knowing where he lives. "

"I don't know where you live," Bemsi said.

"That will be fixed today," Bzinkem said. "I shall pick you up at your home. We shall have a good time. Later we will go to my house after which I will finally drop you home. "

"That will be wonderful," Bemsi said.

"Mind you, we may round up rather late," Bzinkem said.

"No problem with that," replied Bemsi. "In my house, I am in command. "

"See you in the afternoon then," Bzinkem said.

Bzinkem stopped over at his club and had a sumptuous breakfast. There were scrambled eggs on fried potatoes, cottage cheese, bacon, harm and bread, and wonderful kola coffee to wash it down with. One of the good things Satan did for his friends was to give them a good appetite for everything including women and food. This went along with good health and for those who wanted to remain trim, the potential of mucking down excessive fats, proteins, and carbohydrates without gaining useless weight. There were a few obese and shapeless followers of Satan but this was because for specific reasons they wanted to be like that. Body parts and blood were delicious, no doubt, but they were available only during rituals and on special demonic occasions.

After breakfast, Bzinkem decided to go home and take a short nap. Sunday was a day off for domestic staff, but the cook always came in the morning to prepare food for the day. It was not a difficult task as Bzinkem was alone and hardly ever brought home guests. He slept soundly for two hours and got up feeling hungry again. He went to the kitchen, brought out his lunch, and ate with a lot of appetite. After digesting the food with cognac, he switched on the TV and relaxed. He was waiting for departure time.

At thirty minutes past three, he went out to one of his cars and drove out. Bemsi had told his wife that his friend was coming to take him out and was waiting anxiously. Just then Bzinkem drove up in an expensive Mercedes and honked loudly from the road. Bemsi jumped up.

"My friend has come," he said to his wife.

"You make friends with such big rich men?" his wife asked.

"What did you think?" asked Bemsi. "That I will remain small forever?"

Bemsi got out of the house, rushed to the car and joined Bzinkem.

"You could have at least come into the house," Bemsi said. "My wife

would have loved to meet a big and important man like you. "

"Don't worry, there is always time," Bzinkem said.

"So where are we going?" Bemsi asked.

"To a place where there are lots of beautiful women," Bzinkem said calmly.

"Women?" Bemsi asked. "But everybody thinks you are a very respectable man and that frivolities like chasing after women do not interest you. "

"With my money and status," Bzinkem said, "women chase after me. I have to be very strong willed to keep them away. "

"I wish it were like that with me," Bemsi said. "I always have this urge to go after them but get rejected too often. "

"Would you like to have them at your beck and call?" Bzinkem asked.

"Certainly," Bemsi replied. "I would be the happiest person on earth if

I could have beautiful women chatting me up. "

"There is a possibility," Bzinkem said.

"Is there?" Bemsi asked. "Please, help me. "

"You simply need to make much money," Bzinkem said. "Drive a good car like myself, dress smartly, and give lavishly. "

"That is just the problem," Bemsi said. "I earn a very small salary. "

"We can fix that," Bzinkem said. "But first, let's relax and enjoy ourselves. Today is Sunday, remember?"

Bzinkem drove to a sports complex where a female handball team was practicing. The women looked very cute in their scanty attire, and their movements were graceful. After watching for a while, Bzinkem took Bemsi across to the basketball pitch. Here the women were taller and cuter and their brief sportswear exposed a lot of smooth laps and lean stomachs. Over at the volley ball pitch it was the same. Bemsi was so worked up that he almost forgot himself.

Bzinkem brought him back.

"Many of these women take their bath in the gymnasium and change into track suits, but they still look very sexy in those. Then they pass through the bar next door for a drink before they go home. That is where you easily trap them, but to do that, you start by offering a drink, you talk big, offer a lift etc. "

"They are wonderful," Bemsi said. "All beautiful and young. "

"And mostly spinsters, too," Bzinkem said.

"Whew. How did you discover this place?" Bemsi asked.

"When you have money and time you can discover anything," Bzinkem said. "Now, let's move over to the bar. "

They took drinks and sat on high stools next to the counter. Apart from drinks there were lots of nice snacks available. Enough bait to fish for pretty birds.

Despite his age, Bzinkem looked resplendent and attractive. He was dressed in an expensive T-shirt, quality white trousers, expensive tennis shoes, and a cute cap. This appearance earned him a smile from many of the ladies who passed by; meanwhile Bemsi was boiling with lust.

Bzinkem beckoned at two tall, strikingly beautiful girls.

"Would you like to share a drink with us, young ladies?" Bzinkem asked.

"We would love to," one of them answered. "But not perched on those high seats like call girls. "

"We could move to the table over there," Bzinkem said.

He strode over to the free table he had indicated and gallantly pulled out chairs for the ladies. He sat down and placed the keys of his expensive car on the table for all to see.

"My name is Bzinkem," he said, "and my friend here is Bemsi. "

"We thought he was your driver," one of the ladies said. "There is a marked difference between the two of you. "

"What difference?" Bzinkem asked.

"You may be much older, but you have class and all it takes," the other lady said.

"Any woman would fall for you instantly. " Her friend said "Your friend, on the other hand, lacks all the required qualities. "

"You could still polish him up somehow. " Bzinkem said. "A man is just what you make of him. "

After an hour the ladies were ready to go and left their phone contacts with Bzinkem, virtually taking no notice of Bemsi.

"Money speaks in this world," Bemsi said.

"It does," agreed Bzinkem.

It was already dark as they drove into Bzinkem's yard and parked.

"Wow!" said Bemsi admiringly as he stepped out of the car. "This is something. "

They went into the house and into the sitting room.

"How did you acquire all this?" Bemsi asked.

"Well, I did not rob a bank," Bzinkem replied. "I made some efforts"

"I am sure all your children are abroad," Bemsi said. "But where is your wife?"

"She died seven years ago along with my children," Bzinkem replied.

"Yes, I heard something like that. That was before you came to this town, right?" Bemsi asked.

"Yes. It is quite some time. "

"Are you sure you did not sell them for all this wealth?" Bemsi asked.

"What?" Bzinkem said

"I am sorry," replied Bemsi "I did not mean it. I was just joking. "

"So?" Bzinkem said.

"You see this belief in what they call *Musoh*…" Bemsi said.

"What is *Musoh*?" Bzinkem asked.

"*Musoh* is a secret cult into which a man can get initiated. Others call it *Nyongo*. As a member of one of these secret cults, a man may offer his parents, his wife, his children, or all of them for ritual sacrifice to gain fabulous wealth. Some powerful cult members may offer even persons with whom they have no blood relations. These sacrificed persons die mysteriously, and their donor is rewarded with wealth, intelligence, or success. "

"Would you get involved in this kind of thing to get rich?" Bzinkem asked guardedly.

"I don't understand you," Bemsi said.

"Would you give up your wife or children to this kind of cult to get rich and have all the money and women you wanted?"

"Those are devilish acts," Bemsi said. "You forget that I am a fervent Christian like you. Besides, who would want to give up his wife and children just for money?"

"What if it did not involve killing your wife or children?" Bzinkem asked.

"You mean making the same kind of wealth without having to offer my wife or children for ritual sacrifices?" Bemsi asked.

"Yes," Bzinkem replied simply.

"Is that possible?" Bemsi asked.

"Quite possible," Bzinkem said. "In this case, however, you simply switch over from worshiping God to serving Satan."

"You can't be serious," Bemsi said.

"You see," Bzinkem said, "I have been observing you quite closely for a while now and I think I know your desires, your needs, and your problems. If you accept and do what I ask you, I could solve your problems."

"Without hurting my family?" Bemsi wanted to be sure.

"Without touching even a strand of hair on any of them. They will rather participate in enjoying your new found wealth. Just think. Your wife could wear the best clothes any woman could dream of, your children could go to the best schools, and the whole family could have a revered status in society. What else do you want?"

"Even if I have to dine with the devil to become as rich as you are, and on those conditions, I would not hesitate to accept," Bemsi said.

Bzinkem smiled. He had picked the right candidate.

"In fact, you may have to do just that," Bzinkem said.

"Dine with the devil?" Bemsi asked, surprised. He had heard many stories about the devil and his works on earth, but they had all sounded like fairy tales to him.

"I will initiate you into the cult of Diavolo, and you will never lack in your life."

Bemsi realized he was stepping into something dangerous. He had actually been wondering why Bzinkem, who was right up there, had been paying so much interest in him.

"What does this initiation entail?" he asked guardedly.

"Not much," Bzinkem replied. "You will not need to sacrifice anybody. Your wife and children shall all remain alive to share in your new affluence. "

Bemsi considered the situation. So Bzinkem's source of wealth had been Lucifer all along. And the man was a fervent church member and very respectable person in society. He could live like that too.

"I might consider it," he said finally. "What is the initiation ceremony like and who does it?"

"I have the powers to do it," Bzinkem said. "If you are ready, I can do it right now and here. "

Satan never gave you time to rethink or reconsider once you were in his grasp.

"I am ready," Bemsi said.

"Okay then," said Bzinkem. "It won't take long. But note that anything that has to do with Satan involves blood and sex. "

Bzinkem went to a special cupboard and brought out two very small clay cups. Each cup could contain about two table spoons full of blood. From the cupboard he also brought out a syringe.

Then he opened another cupboard where a strange looking TV set lodged inside. He switched on the TV and a homosexual couple started performing.

"Now," said Bzinkem. "I will drink a wee bit of your blood and you will drink a little of mine. Through this, you would have entered a blood pact with Lucifer himself. "

"Are you a demon?" Bemsi asked.

"I am a fiend," Bzinkem said. "There are many of us on earth who are servants of Lucifer and recruit for him. "

"So I also become a fiend after this initiation?" Bemsi asked in great fright.

59

"You simply become a follower of Lucifer," Bzinkem replied. "But as a follower, you will have all the riches you want. However, you will live like a normal man and die like a normal man. The degree of evil you get involved in will determine whether you will continue living after death as a real fiend. "

"There is a life after death involved?" Bemsi asked.

"Yes. I started out as an ordinary man and lived in Madagascar where I was recruited as a follower of Satan. I had a family just like you and lived my normal life with them although I was a simple servant of Satan. I discarded my normal human body some five hundred years ago and since then have continued living as a fiend. I have lived in many countries and many cities of Africa. You see, what Satan gives us is life here on earth, packed full with enjoyment and freedom, not some dull life in heaven, full of control and restrictions. "

"But Satan and his followers are supposed to be in hell where there is fire, weeping, and gnashing of teeth," Bemsi said.

"That is how people get misled by God and his lackeys," Bzinkem said. "Hell is Satan's abode where he retires once in a while to a solitary life, but his kingdom is actually on earth and all his followers are here. There is no raging fire that burns Satan and his followers eternally. "

"So the issue of hell fire is just a sham?"

"It is simply the immeasurable evil that is considered as fire. The sorrow, weeping, and gnashing of teeth on earth is the lot of the fools who cling to God and reject Satan. Satan, on the other hand, gives his followers everything on earth. You have long life, wealth, lots of sexual enjoyment, and the right to do whatever you want. "

"I never saw it like that," Bemsi said.

"Think well," Bzinkem said. "Instead of relaxing in your bed, you get up early to go to church. You give up part of your meagre income to the church. And what could be more boring than those long prayers and novenas? And then there is fasting. During some periods, you abandon good food and drinks and fast. Satan allows you to relax, to enjoy fully, without sacrificing anything or giving up any earthly pleasure. "

"But you go to church," Bemsi pointed out.

"For a purpose," Bzinkem said. "But it ends there. I go only on Sundays, and the money I give there is just a minute part of what Satan gives me. Apart from that, I don't fast, I don't pray, and I don't involve myself in any boring church activity. "

"So what will Satan give to me if I am initiated, and how do I satisfy him?"

"You will become successful in everything you do and become wealthy. As I told you, Satan does not promise you some imaginary super life in heaven. He makes you enjoy everything right here. To please him, do evil things as often as possible. You don't need to expose them. Go after people's wives and daughters. You could destroy small boys homosexually, cheat wherever and whenever you can. Kill when possible, so long as it will not be discovered. The more evil you do, the more Satan will be satisfied with you. "

Bzinkem picked up the syringe drew blood from a vein in his left arm and put it in one of the clay cups which he gave Bemsi to drink. Bemsi frowned, closed his eyes, threw the reddish liquid into his mouth and gulped. With the same syringe, Bzinkem drew blood from Bemsi and drank from the other clay cup.

The carnal act on the TV screen was going on but did not seem to be of any interest to Bemsi. Bemsi loved sex, but his passion was for women not men. He had never imagined himself indulging in such a strange act where two bulls or cocks are struggling to copulate.

"Now is the next step," Bzinkem said. "I put on the homosexual pornographic film to prepare you for this and ascertain your tendencies. From every indication you are not gay and are not excited at all by homosexual displays. However, we are both men, you who are being initiated and me who is initiating you. A carnal relationship is inevitable in all satanic rituals so you will offer me your anal body orifice and take advantage of mine after. "

Bemsi was horrified. He had thought the pornographic scenes on the TV screen were all about the sexual act to accompany the rituals.

Bzinkem was already undressing and urged him to do same. Undressed there was nothing feminine about Bzinkem. Everything about him was quite masculine. Although the texture of his skin was good enough for an elderly good looking man, it was quite hairy and far from the kind of smooth female skin that attracts you to want to caress it. Bemsi could have coped better with one of the lady boys of Bangkok or the she-males from Brazil.

Bemsi looked with apprehension as Bzinkem finally stripped completely naked. Bzinkem was well endowed with the male sexual organ and the idea of being penetrated by it was frightening. Since he had already come that far, however, he took a large sip of brandy, closed his eyes, and submitted himself for the ritual.

At the end of the initiation, Bemsi was feeling quite sore around the anal region. Apart from some rare occasions when egesting became difficult because of large hard stool, nothing as big as Bzinkem's sexual organ had ever gone close to his rectum. He was equally disgusted with the fact that he had to go into a man.

"You are now a follower and servant of Satan," Bzinkem said. "You will now have a comfortable life, lots of riches, women, and whatever you like. "

"Thank you very much," Bemsi finally managed to say.

"But," Bzinkem continued, "to serve Satan you must give up God. You may continue to attend mass on Sundays, however, so as to give the impression that nothing has changed. "

"I understand," Bemsi said.

"Good," Bzinkem said. "Avoid making the sign of the cross completely and never go close to the altar again. There are some forces there that might harm you. "

"I will always stay at the back," Bemsi said. "I now understand why you are always on the last pew at the back of the church. "

"I see you are getting it," Bzinkem said. "Don't touch holy water again and no more communion. "

"That is understood, too. " Bemsi said.

"Finally," Bzinkem said. "Avoid touching things like the Rosary, the Bible, and other holy objects. "

"It is quite clear," Bemsi said.

"You are a free man now," Bzinkem said, "no longer tied to long boring novenas and prayers to God. You don't need to fast or give up anything during lent. "

"There are no prayers to Satan?" asked Bemsi.

"With Satan, you simply need to do something evil," Bzinkem said. "Whenever you want to please him, do some evil deed, like adultery, which you will enjoy and which will now be very easy with all your money and power. "

By the time Bzinkem dropped Bemsi at his home, it was already past midnight. Bemsi's wife quietly opened the door to let her husband in and was surprised that he was not roaring drunk. He rather looked quiet and submissive as he moved straight to the bedroom.

Bzinkem turned the vehicle and drove off. This was a satisfied senior fiend. He had accomplished his yearly recruitment of a follower of Satan who, if well groomed, could eventually become an actual fiend and maybe even rise up to the position of a senior friend.

Bemsi had been a relatively easy catch. With some tough cases, you had to use devilish powers to make them suffer like Job in the Bible. You confronted them with such a gruelling ordeal that would make them ready to accept any way out and become prepared to do anything to relieve them of the suffering. Then you offered them solace from Satan and a wonderfully comfortable life devoid of any suffering. There, you were guaranteed of acceptance without any hesitation. There were very few who could resist to the end like Job.

5

Bzinkem got up in the morning looking very fresh and happy. He had come back the previous evening from one of his regular orgies and still felt fully satisfied. As he was cleaning his teeth, his phone rang. It was not the usual ring from ordinary humans but some peculiar eerie sound. He understood at once that it was the Grand Fiend and rushed to answer it. The Grand Fiend was a nasty fellow, quick to anger, and hardly ever forgiving.

"Yes, Most Evil Lord?" Bzinkem answered.

"Bzinkem," Grand Fiend said, "it will soon be the feast of Diavolo and, as usual, we of the inner core of the congregation of fiends are supposed to hold our planning meeting at Beelzebub's place. I have programmed the meeting for this coming Friday at midnight. No late coming shall be tolerated. "

"I have heard you, Most Evil Lord," Bzinkem said.

"I have reserved ten humans for our entertainment," the Grand Fiend said. "That will be enough for the few of us. As you know, only those who have direct access to our master Satan are invited to the meeting. "

"Thanks, O Most Evil Lord," Bzinkem said. "I thirst for blood already. I hope there will be enough fiend whores. We hardly have access to them except on such occasions, and they are a lot more interesting than human females. "

Such meetings of fiends often ended up with sexual orgies.

"Sure," replied the Grand Fiend. "Jezebel has been asked to rally several pretty things for our pleasure. You shall have your fill. "

65

"See you then, Most Evil Lord," Bzinkem said. "And may Satan keep you in perfect shape for the occasion. "

The strange phone conversation was over. Like Christmas and other feasts on earth that are celebrated widely, the fiends held the feast of Diavolo every ten years. This was celebrated in the various continents with gory feasts, and praises to Satan rent the air during these occasions. The African fiends generally met somewhere in the Sahara desert and feasted for three days. Preparations for this feast were carried out by an inner core of senior fiends like Bzinkem and it was to one of these preparatory meetings that he had been invited by the Grand Fiend.

The thought of meeting old friends was exciting. Even more exciting was the promise of meeting actual female friends. Lovemaking with female fiends was always hectic and full of a combination of lust, sadism, and unimaginable orgasms. You always ended up with bruises all over your back and even on your face, but it was worth it.

Bzinkem's next few days were occupied by preparations for the meeting. The grand fiend was supposed to prepare a speech to present during the feast of Diavolo and would have to collect information for this speech from reports that senior fiends would present. Satan appeared here and there, whenever he was invoked, but lacked God's ability to be everywhere at the same time and to know everything. He had to rely on the Grand Fiends in the various continents to be able to have thorough knowledge of what was transpiring all over the world.

Bzinkem had to make sure that his outfit for the meeting was in good condition. You did not go to the Grand Fiend's meetings dressed just anyhow. The African Fiends normally wore grey cloaks on top of their suits, with tall, grey hats perched on their heads. Bzinkem checked the grey tie that was supposed to go with the grey suit and white shirt. There were no female senior fiends as females were simply considered necessary companions to the male fiends. There was, therefore, no official dressing code for them apart from the fact that they were supposed to dress as sexily as possible when invited, to provide pleasure to the male fiends.

Bzinkem's special attire was always kept in some inner section of his wardrobe, away from the ordinary house help. After being satisfied that the items were all in good form, he placed them back in their secret cache and went to bed.

The day of the meeting with the Grand Fiend finally arrived. Bzinkem ate very little during the day. He was now sitting in the living room, waiting for eleven pm, the take-off time, while sipping a glass of dry martini. They generally did not provide aperitifs in fiend gatherings. He kept looking at the clock on the wall to make sure that he would not miss a minute. When it was ten o'clock, he went to his room, pulled out his suit for the occasion, and got dressed. His shoes and socks were also grey.

Bzinkem reached into the special section in the wardrobe again and pressed a switch. Immediately, a small, disguised door opened on one of the walls and a flight of stairs showed. Bzinkem stepped out, climbed the stairs to a skylight which he opened to climb out on the roof. Out on the roof, he surveyed the night sky and observed the weather. The weather was quite good for night flights. Bzinkem stretched out his hands and was immediately transformed into a huge owl. He flapped his wings a few times, flew off from the roof, and headed for Beelzebub's place where the meeting was programmed to be held.

Unlike other senior fiends, Beelzebub did not live in a mansion disguised as an ordinary human citizen. Beelzebub had opted to live in a huge castle, away from all humanity, and planted somewhere in the deserts of Niger. No human had ever set foot here, and from the air, it appeared to all who cared to look down from the plane like some strange sand dune.

Transformed into an owl, Bzinkem flew very fast, and in just an hour's time, was circulating over Beelzebub's castle looking for the landing pad. The landing pad was a platform by a huge open window. There were other owls coming in to land, so Bzinkem slowed down and flew carefully to the landing pad. It was designed for birds, so you had to jump from the pad into the room before you transformed back into your real form.

There were a handful of senior fiends already present and more were still arriving. Bzinkem smiled as he recognized the other fiends; but, according to protocol, he moved up to Grand Fiend first and bowed. The Grand Fiend acknowledged the greeting, tapping him on the back. Bzinkem then moved to the host of the meeting. Beelzebub was discussing something with Jezebel, probably arranging for entertainment after the meeting. Actually, such meetings did not last long. What took up much of the time was the accompanying orgy, so Jezebel's role was quite important. Beelzebub turned and shook hands with Bzinkem, told him to feel free, and continued his discussion with Jezebel. Bzinkem now felt free to move round and greet the other fiends. The room was lit by huge candles and a blazing fire at the grate. Despite the ample size of the room, a quarter of a whole wall was covered with a large picture of Satan.

Beelzebub surely wanted to prove to all visitors that his worship for Lucifer was not in half measures.

All the hideous features of Lucifer's face came out in the portrait picture and gave the impression that he was watching every step of his faithful followers. A vicious serpent, the animal sacred to Lucifer, was also pictured on the rest of the wall. The serpent had wrapped a helpless human in its folds and was about to devour him. There were pictures of other animals linked to dark arts like the vampire bat, the owl, the wolf and the vulture. Different forms of sexual acts between wild looking fiends, between ware wolves and between humans were represented on part of another wall, while vivid scenes of bloody sacrifices and other frightful activities covered the rest of the wall. Beelzebub was really imaginative and this room was quite representative of all that fiends indulged in.

At twelve midnight an eerie sound came from a strange caged animal that served as a clock for Beelzebub and immediately, the window through which the senior fiends had flown in closed. Any late comer would be blocked from entering and his high status as senior fiend would be lost. However, all the senior African fiends were present, forty of them. They all took their seats and settled down to wait for the Grand Fiend to address them.

"All of you are welcome here," Beelzebub said. "I hope you will all have a great time in my home. "

"Thanks, Beelzebub," the Grand Fiend said. "We are happy that you always provide this most appropriate home for the meeting of senior fiends. We are all looking forward to our orgy so we shall be brief with the meeting proper. "

The Grand Fiend looked towards the wall where Lucifer's gigantic portrait was.

"Let's start by giving honour to our great master, Lucifer.
"

All the fiends turned towards the portrait.

"Oh, master of hell and evil," the Grand Fiend continued, "we thank you for this long life which we are enjoying right here on earth. It is only you who makes it possible. We prefer this free and luxurious life right here and now to any everlasting life promised by God - not here on earth but in some imaginary abode called heaven. If one could even imagine how this heaven would be: no bloody drinks, no alcohol, no hard drugs, no sex, and no crime and evil. It would really be a dull life. We are happy with you Satan, and will always remain your servants. "

"Lord of darkness and evil," all the others chorused in worship.

"Now," said Grand Fiend, "let us move to the next topic. Each senior fiend shall shove his report into the reception box there. "

The fiends all went and dropped some strange looking balls into the box. Their reports were contained in these objects.

"Next item," the Grand Fiend said. "Feast of Diavolo will be held at the usual place in the Libyan desert. The worship of the great Lucifer shall be followed by a great feast as usual. We must therefore mobilize palatable human parts, like the liver, the kidney, and the lungs. We know that, on this occasion, the hearts and the genitals are reserved for the dark priests and for our master Lucifer. We will have to arrange how all these items will get to our feasting tables. Before, it was quite easy. Caravans of travellers on camel back were easily diverted to our feasting site and their entrails ended up on our tables. Today, earthlings mostly use vehicles and planes, so we are compelled to make special efforts to fill our larder for the feast. I will assign each of you with the task of providing victuals for the feast. For this year, Sakarabru, Nyamabo, Bzinkem, Ngvumissi, Shabriri, Set, Wele Gumaliand Bousbir will supply the body organs required. "

Supplying body organs did not mean that you openly murdered humans and extracted the organs to supply at the venue of the feast. That would be rather complicated. Besides, the organs had to be eaten fresh. Fiends were very particular about the state of the offal they feasted on, and the slightest indication that the stuff was stale resulted in total rejection. What actually happened was that each senior fiend assigned to provide the body organs arranged for ghastly accidents in his country and each country had one senior fiend with such powers. Bus accidents and a few other accidents influenced by these fiends that ended in the death of most of the passengers served as a form of transmission. The bodies of the deceased passengers remained but thorough examination of the corpses would have proven the disappearance of the internal body organs in which the fiends were interested. The system of extraction of these parts and their transportation to the feasting area was a complicated and intricate process. Invisible goblins hacked open the victims, extracted the parts and sealed up the cut expertly. This took them less than a minute. The parts were carried in huge plastic bags and flown by invisible crows to the desert.

"Let's talk about drinks now," the Grand Fiend said. "This year we want to make a difference. We want to have real variety. So far our variety was limited to a choice between Chinese blood, Eskimo blood, Quicha blood, Pygmy blood etc. This time we shall go further. Like the humans who have varieties ranging from different types of sparkling wine, white wine, red wine, or port wine, to whiskeys, cognacs, gins, and vermouths, we want to increase our range. We shall have human blood, of course, and, to that, add goat, camel, baboon, and springbok blood. What do you think?"

"Could any other blood taste better than human blood?" Beelzebub asked.

"It is a matter of choice," the Grand Fiend said. "While some humans think that there is nothing better than whiskey, others prefer fruit juice, beer, or wine. These are drinks of vast varieties."

"I agree with you," said an Arab fiend from Libya. "Camel blood, for example, is quite wonderful."

"Have you ever tasted the blood of a he-goat?" Bzinkem's neighbour asked him. "It has an odd smell, but is quite nice and could act like a sexual stimulant."

"You left out birds," another fiend said. "Vulture blood is wonderful. Many female fiends like it."

This was a fiend from Sudan.

"What of elephant blood?" Bzinkem asked "One elephant could give much to drink."

However, it appeared that no fiend had ever bothered to drink elephant blood so no opinion was given.

"Out of those that I did not yet assign, these ten will provide blood from various animals," said the Grand Fiend. "Chemosit, you will head this team. The rest of the senior fiends here will provide human blood. Congo Zandor shall lead that team."

The Grand Fiend beckoned Beelzebub and whispered something to him, then turned round to the other fiends.

"Time has come for the part that I am sure interests all of you most," the Grand Fiend said. "Beelzebub has provided fresh liver, spleen, and lungs for everybody. Since we shall have female fiends feasting with us, the hearts and genitals shall not be openly displayed. Those interested in these items should collect them from Beelzebub himself. There is enough blood to drink. Relax. Have your fill and take as many female fiends as you can have. "

"We shall all move into the orgy room," Beelzebub said. . . "The orgy and sex acts shall be open and competitive. "

The senior fiends moved expectantly into the orgy room where the feast and the female friends were waiting. What took place in the room can only be properly narrated by another fiend. However, it is understood that all the fiends left thoroughly satisfied and satiated.

The feast of Diavolo was always the most celebrated day in the lives of the fiends. They all acquired a new set of teeth and new eyes that would last them for the next ten years. That way they always had very sharp teeth and sharp eyes. The feast was celebrated by all fiends and during these feasts, new recruits were enlisted.

On this day, feasts were held in all the continents: Asia, Europe, North America, South America, Australia and Africa. Thanks to the time difference between continents, Satan appeared in all of them and spent at least thirty minutes feasting on special human parts reserved for him and gave the fiends his blessings.

On the eve of the feast of Diavolo, at midnight, Bzinkem dressed up in his devil suit, went up to his roof, and flew off in the form of an owl. He flew fast and soon landed at his destination. Beelzebub was already there with a handful of other senior fiends and other fiends kept flying in. They were now waiting for the Grand Fiend to arrive. Soon there was the flap of heavy wings as the Grand Fiend circled and landed. He was holding a Bible in his left hand and a thick black cloth in his right hand. The other fiends crowded around him, and he led them up a small sand dune. At the top, he wrapped the Bible well in the thick black cloth and dropped it on the ground.

He placed his left foot on the Bible, raised up his hands, and shouted.

"Oh, master Lucifer, the feast of Diavolo has come, the feast during which we simulate your conquest and overthrow of God. God may think that he is powerful, but no! Satan shall one day sit on that great throne and rule over the whole world. You shall no longer be simply master of darkness but shall rule even during daylight. In short, your stealthy efforts in the dark shall become audacious even during the day."

The Grand Fiend moved his left foot on the Bible as if he were crushing it.

"This is God's book under my left foot," the Grand Fiend said. "just as God shall end up under your feet. We shall go even further and bury this horrid book they call Bible in simulation of how you shall destroy and put God away."

Beelzebub, Sakarabruand Chemosit dug a hole in the sand, and the Grand Fiend buried the Bible in it. They all took turns in stamping upon the spot where the Bible had been buried and, after this strange ceremony, moved over to another dune where the official part of the feast of Diavolo would be celebrated. Five men and five women were strapped to a crude table and would soon be sacrificed. Live offerings to Satan were common. The Grand Fiend took a sharp knife and sliced off the first man's penis. As the man howled in pain, the Grand Fiend threw the penis into his mouth and stared chewing with his sharp teeth. As the man was writhing

74

in pain, he went over to the first woman and sliced off one of her breast, which he handed over to Beelzebub. Then he sliced off the other and handed it to Chemosit. As these too started chewing on the body parts, the Grand Fiend went back to the man and cut off the testicles. They were now quite covered with blood but he ate them with relish. He then expertly cut open the men and women and instructed the other fiends to eat the internal organs. When this bloody meal was over, they moved to a set of benches where there were several kegs of blood and wooden cups. The senior fiends spent their whole night in the open, enjoying their bloody wine.

Just before sun rise, each senior fiend transformed into an owl, clapped his wings and took off for his home.

Back home on the day of the Feast of Diavolo, Bzinkem pressed a switch disguised on one of the walls in his bedroom and a screen appeared. He waved his hands in front of it and images came on. With his mind, he switched from image to image and finally settled on a bus that was cruising at breakneck speed to some far destination. Although it was built to carry seventy passengers, there were many more persons inside. As they approached an oncoming petrol tanker, Bzinkem planted his thumb on the windscreen in the image.

The driver of the bus, who had been concentrating on the road with much attention because of the speed and numbers he was transporting, suddenly could not see in front. It would appear some huge black object had settled on the windscreen. He stepped on the breaks but it was too late as the bus skidded with screeching tires and crashed into the oncoming petrol tanker. The impact was devastating. More than half of the passengers that the bus was transporting died immediately. The others were trapped in the wreckage, most of them unconscious. Soon, there was a large explosion followed by roaring fire as the volatile liquid that the tanker was carrying was released.

Bzinkem roared into sinister laughter as he observed the carnage he had just caused. With his fiend eyes, he could see the goblins carry away the entrails of the dead humans that they had succeeded in extracting before the fire consumed everything.

Bzinkem searched again for a little while and came across another bus that had gathered speed and was about to bypass a lorry. As he jabbed his thumb against the screen just where the windscreen of the bus was supposed to be, he observed closely for results. The driver of the bus realized suddenly that a huge object had blocked his view. This was a very experienced driver and he stepped slightly on the brakes while veering off slightly to his side and away from the oncoming vehicle. The bus continued into the bush and was eventually caught by thick brush. Some passengers were injured but there were no deaths.

Bzinkem sighed in disappointment and continued searching. He came across another bus, filled to the brim and descending a steep hill with care. Bzinkem looked with concentration and wished the brakes would fail. They did, and the bus gathered speed beyond the control of the driver. The bus eventually crashed into a ravine; and the little goblins went to work extracting and ferrying away body parts.

Bzinkem was successfully providing food for the feast of Diavolo.

A few more attempts resulted in the crashing of three more buses. About two hundred humans had been sacrificed and their entrails spiritually transferred to the desert for the feast of Diavolo.

The Feast of Diavolo was really a grand affair. Apart from the senior fiends all dressed in grey, there were junior fiends that were now aspiring to be upgraded into senior fiends. This was just the occasion when it happened. To be upgraded into a senior fiend did not come that easy. Fiends rarely died, and most of the time, fiends were upgraded in replacement of a departed senior fiend. The lowest class here was comprised of witches and wizards.

Voodoo adherents were mostly found around Latin America and Vampires were either in America or Europe. In Russia, there were Vaidemas, Fokusnics and the followers of Chernobog. Other parts of the world had their own class of witches and wizards.

Also attending the African feast of Diavolo were members of certain evil secret cults like the *Famlah, Nyongo,* and *Mussoh.* These cult members mainly sacrificed relatives for riches, their intention being to belong to the wealthy class. During their feasts, they fed on human flesh and drank blood. As for the wizards and witches, they also fed on human flesh and drank blood, but instead of wealth, they were rather interested in mystical powers Which they used to do evil things - kill, frustrate the progress of others, maim, cause bareness in women and immeasurable sorrow. . The wizards and witches were thus generally among the poor and simply enjoyed the havoc they committed on others. Members of the Famlah, Musso, and Nyongo, on the other hand, were wealthy business men who only harmed other humans when their turn to provide a human being for sacrifice arrived. Some of them were actually "good" ladies and gentlemen

77

who donated generously to charity, led exemplary lives, and were strong practicing Christians.

All these classes of servants of Satan were present, including Bemsi, Bzinkem's latest recruit. Bemsi marvelled at the type of people he saw. Although they were from all over Africa, he could spot quite a few renowned politicians, tycoons, and professors that he knew or had read about, not only from his own town and country, but from all over Africa. . These were people you would never have imagined as followers of Satan.

Bemsi saw Bzinkem among the senior fiends gathered around the huge altar. There were six live humans there to be sacrificed to Satan. Barrels of assorted blood, including animal blood, were stacked at one corner ready to be served when the time came. Bemsi was still learning how to enjoy drinking blood in place of wine. However, it looked like once initiated, your taste buds immediately developed the inkling for blood; Bemsi found himself already thirsty for it. Heaps of fresh liver, lungs, spleen, and intestines were also available while male genitals, female breasts, and hearts were reserved for the senior fiends.

The previous night, the senior fiends had launched the feast of Diavolo with their ritual desecration of God's book. During the feast itself, and in the presence of Satan, they were going to soak a copy of the Bible in blood and transform all the chapters and verses into a bloody paper paste. That would be the climax of the feast of Diavolo.

Suddenly, there was loud thunder and Satan appeared. He made his way to the altar where the Grand Fiend received him and placed him on a high chair. The feast began with the immolation of the six persons on the altar. There were three men and three women and all the male genitals and female breasts were handed over to Satan. Then the Grand Fiend and a few colleagues ate the hearts.

The Grand Fiend then read his speech in honour of Satan. It was fiery, heaped praises on Satan, and gave a brief run down on their achievements. Satan smiled broadly as he listened and chewed on his meat. At the end of the speech, female friends came out and served meat and blood for all to eat and drink. There were lots of ambiance and hearty conversations.

Then a list of candidates that had qualified to be raised into senior fiends was called, and they all came out and lined up in front of the altar. There were three of them, all dressed in brown suits and cloaks.

The bloody paper paste that had once been a copy of the Bible was brought and rubbed on the soles of their shoes. They were now supposed to be tougher than God's word. The Grand Fiend opened a bluish box and brought out a Rosary.

"This," the Grand Fiend said, "is supposed to be a simple object, developed to assist Christians to call on the intercession of this woman they claim is holy in order to get their problems through to God. "

The Grand Fiend cut the string that held the beads together and allowed the beads to fall to the ground and roll in different directions.

"This is what we shall do to those who worship her," he said. "We shall scatter them like chickens without a mother hen. "

The Grand Fiend turned to Satan

"Before her bastard son arrived on the scene, you had been there," he said to Satan "He is trying to undo the evil and destruction you have done throughout the world. And they are insisting on calling him God, too. "

"Ridiculous!" Satan said in anger "After God, it is me. And very soon I will become number one. "

At that moment, there was a loud rumble in the sky and out of the clouds came Angel Michael in his golden chariot. With a loud shriek, Satan disappeared into the ground before the thunderbolts released by Angel Michael hit target. The Grand Fiend and eleven other senior fiends found themselves direct targets, and their bodies sizzled from the burning impact of the thunderbolts. Their charred remains ended up simply as heaps of ash. Angel Michael turned round and disappeared into the clouds.

There was silence and shock among the congregation of fiends and followers of Satan. Once more God had proven that he was stronger without necessarily coming out himself to confront Satan. However, Satan eventually reappeared, looking angry and frustrated.

"Michael!" Satan shouted. "One day I will get you. You just wait. "

Satan examined the carnage that Michael had left behind in his wake.

"Eeeegh," Satan screamed. "I shall destroy him. I shall make mashed potatoes out of him and throw it to the pigs. "

Satan turned to the rest of the senior fiends.

"Don't stand there looking so forlorn," he said. "Chemosit, try to organize things. The feast must continue and these selected fiends must become senior fiends. "

Chemosit rallied Bzinkem and the remaining senior fiends into action. He was aware of the fact that a new Grand Fiend had to be elected, and the mere mention of his name in this circumstance pointed to the fact that he was a possible favourite of Satan.

Fiends do not have human feelings and the demise of the Grand Fiend and some of his peers did not in any way weigh on the consciences of the other fiends and followers of Satan. No appetites were lost, no regrets and no sad feelings lingered. After the three new senior fiends were hugged by the old ones, feasting started. In a short while, all thoughts about what had just transpired, thanks to angel Michael, disappeared.

Satan decided to stay longer so as to fully assert himself after being sorely disgraced by Angel Michael. He even promised to come back for the orgy and reserved Jezebel for partner.

"Before we leave here on the third day," Satan declared before leaving, "we must elect a new Grand Fiend. We shall see about replacing g the other senior fiends that went down with the Grand Fiend, later. "

The third day came with a lot of preparation. There was going to be election of a Grand fiend and all the old senior fiends were eligible. Chemosit, who had been in control since the demise of the Grand fiend, had set up a very powerful rigging machinery and was sure to make it. Bzinkem was no less ambitious. He had created a small following of his admirers and equally put in place his own means of fraud. The senior fiends and their followers were quite ready for a free for all and teeth and claws had been sharpened for the purpose.

As voting was about to start, it was discovered that the ballot boxes were all filled. The first accused was Chemosit and he was actually guilty as sin. But then the boxes were quite full, an indication that he was not the only culprit. Further verification proved that other senior fiends had equally arranged to have the boxes filled with their ballots even before voting started.

It was agreed that the voters should line up behind the candidate of their choice. After counting, it was discovered that Chemosit had the highest number of votes despite the fact that his line was shortest. This resulted into a real brawl that only ended with the arrival of Satan. He noted with much satisfaction the high handed manner in which the election was being handled and praised everybody for behaving like true followers of Satan. Then he went ahead to declare Bzinkem as the democratically elected Grand fiend.

Bzinkem had virtually reached the apex. Becoming a Grand Fiend was a life goal, and the only higher official was the Grand Baron. Becoming a Grand Baron was a far-fetched dream. It was like an African Cardinal, imagining himself elected as Pope. Bzinkem thus considered the position of Grand Fiend as having reached the apex. He was now the highest fiend in Africa.

6

Witches, wizards, cultists, and other servants of Satan were generally married and had families while living their normal lives on earth. Some of them even had large families, which served as animal farms from which they collected human items to offer for ritual sacrifices whenever their turn came or when they needed to replenish their bank accounts.

On the other hand, fiends like Bzinkem who had lived out the normal life that God had given them and now existed thanks to Satan, generally remained unmarried. It was more convenient for them to lead single lives, and they were not permitted to marry mortal women. On the other hand, female fiends were so frivolous and free that no fiend who had the slightest touch of jealousy in him could easily take the risk of developing any intimate relationship with one. However, a few occasions came up where two demon lovers decided that their attachment for each other warranted their getting married.

Marriage between two fiends was always a hectic affair and, like all their occasions, involved a lot of gore and sex. Bzinkem had attended several such marriages but had personally avoided getting too emotional with any female fiend. Female fiends could be as jealous as they were frivolous, and could tear each other up if a female fiend caught another female fiend flirting with her husband.

One night Bzinkem received a fiend call. These calls came through the normal mobile phone but had an eerie ringing tone. The call was an invitation to a fiend wedding in Ghana. That was wonderful. Among the female fiends with whom he had had an affair, the most interesting one was from Ghana. Bzinkem was thus anxiously looking forward to meeting her.

On the day of the wedding, Frimpong, the bridegroom, looked quite handsome in his grey suit. He was a senior fiend, and was respecting their official attire of grey shoes, grey suit, and grey cloak. All the other senior fiends were dressed the same. Echueh, the bride, was a strikingly beautiful fiend who had served as one of Jezebel's team for more than three hundred years and was now prepared to reserve herself for one fiend. She was dressed in a well cut white dress.

The African fiends arrived first, Bzinkem among them. The African fiends had all brought along some support to make the wedding a great event. Among them, Tando Ashanti, Sakarabru, Shabriri, Set, and WeleGumali from Kenya were elected as officials during the occasion.

Weddings were rare and actually attracted fiends from all over. Azrael, the Muslim angel of death, arrived first among guests from out of Africa. Shortly after, the frightening Frankenstein plodded in and was received by the hosts and the African fiends. A delegation comprised of Grand Bois and two *Houngans* accompanied Olisha, a voodoo goddess, and came in from Haiti. When Ikwaokinyapippilele from Panama arrived, every fiend greeted him excitedly and marvelled at his interesting name. More fiends were still coming in. Lebara and Guaricana flew in from Brazil, accompanied by Keron-Kenken from Patagonia and Xic from Guatemala. Mexico was well represented by the Aztec fiend called Tezcatlípoca and a Toltec demon called Tlacatecolototl. Kok-Lir came all the way from Borneo.

Unlike the usual ritual sacrifices and feasts, marriage ceremonies were special and other items apart from gore and body parts were bought in by invitees to brighten the feasting table. Kali and Ravana from India, for example, had brought along chapattis to accompany the raw human flesh. Akop, Bumalin, Xa-Mul and Angul from the Philippines brought some Ourangoutang blood from the East. Apepi from Egypt and Azidahaka from Iran brought some fresh camel blood. Beng from Rumania, and the Slavic demon called Chernobog brought along some vodka to lace their bloody drink with. They were already used to drinking alcoholic blood. Chu Kwai - Sen Chun from China was smoking opium along with his drink of African blood. The plat de resistance for the day was the fresh vampire bats that Dracula had brought along in several containers that looked like coffins. Every fiend wanted to have a taste of the revolting creatures and all praised Dracula for having done well.

The ceremonial part was quite brief as usual with the Grand Fiend of Africa presiding. He was assisted by one of the *Houngans* from Haiti. To tie their bond, the couple performed a sexual act in front of the invitees while the Grand Fiend and the *Houngan* urged them on. After proving to everybody that they could continue as man and wife, the couple took an oath of fidelity and love for one another in front of the Grand Fiend and the *Houngan*. This oath would be tested during the feast and orgy as other fiends would make passes at the bride and the groom would be sorely tempted by attractive sexy female fiends.

Bzinkem was now the Grand Fiend and the centre of attraction. He decided to have real fun and sample rare fiend females instead of the usual African fare. He started with Hecate, the Queen of the witches. He then switched over to Hatu-Atu-Topun and Hetu-Ahin, female demons from Polynesia, and later on to Jahi, a Persian female demon

After such a marriage, the couple made a trip to hell on honeymoon. Satan's abode was a cold, lonely retreat where honeymoon entailed full attention to each other. The only other visitor was Satan himself, who often participated in the sex acts that comprised the principal activities during honeymoon.

7

S atan sat on his cold throne brooding over the continuous humiliation he received from God and Angel Michael. He was once a favourite angel, considered virtually as a son of God. He could have still been there now, and this fellow Jesus would have been nowhere near him. Greed had pushed him to act hastily, and God had discovered early enough that he had harmful ambitions and could not be trusted. If it had been another angel, God might simply have destroyed him with fire; but, being almost like a son to Him, God had withheld his total destruction. Was it actually his own powers that had prevented God from destroying him? But where did the powers come from?

Satan rubbed his forehead and looked round his lonely palace. No laughter, no company, no music, and no nectar to drink. In an attempt to keep heaven even livelier, there were Cherubim and Seraphim who provided music and laughter. Satan, on the other hand, had other forms of these same things. He had thousands of albums of sexy music and rap music, full of obscenities. He had all forms of obscene dances and performances. In place of cherubim and seraphim, he had ghouls, goblins, hob goblins, sabbat demons, Djinns, furies, banshees, you name them. He had all these on earth anyway, but nothing in hell.

Just like every great leader, Satan had a host of senior aides, all fallen angels that had joined him in the rebellion against God. Many among them were Generals, all commanding armies of lost souls. The mode of recruitment into these armies was simple. While you were still alive and lived on earth you were lured by Lucifer's agents to live and die in sin. After death, you had no other place to go but enlist into Lucifer's army. With the millions that have been dying on earth, and quite a good percentage of them sinners, the army was indeed a large one. However, God had a strong army commander in Michael, assisted by strong Generals like Raphael. Despite his large army, Satan was still happy each time he hit below the belt and succeeded in getting a soul away from God.

Unlike in heaven, where there was general communion of saints and where everybody lived happily around God, Satan's generals and high officials, though also in hell, lived in isolation from each other and only came together during their unending strategic meetings against God and heaven. Satan was also obliged to stay alone and gnash his teeth at his constant failure to defeat God. In this situation, his mind was constantly full of evil plans that would take him closer to his target.

What puzzled him was God's soft spot for him. Was God actually using him to make the world realize the need for Godly protection? If there was no evil on earth, then there would be no reason to adore God or seek God's protection. Yes, God always enjoyed himself thoroughly and felt very happy and satisfied each time a sinner repented and came begging for forgiveness, and that would not happen if he, Satan was not there to lead them into sin. Apart from that, God loved being considered as a saviour and a protector. He needed a very bad and evil force from which to protect the people of the earth, thus showing that he was a very useful God. God had given him much more power than other angels. He had even succeeded in transforming Lilith, the first wife of Adam, before Eve, into a demon. And when God had replaced Lilith with Eve, he had still succeeded in enabling

Leviathan, a Grand Admiral of Hell, to seduce Adam and Eve.

Satan recalled lots of evil things that he had done which could have been nipped in the bud or quashed outright by God if he had wanted to. He remembered the various occasions where God had actually allowed him to tempt good fellows like Job. God had even put that presumptuous Jesus, who claimed to have come closer to God than Satan when he was still in heaven, at his disposal. Maybe God had been using him all along and he had foolishly been tagging along.

But then, he was Lucifer, the master of all evil, who thrived on evil and lived for evil. His main goal was to turn the world into an evil place ruled by him where God would have no place. Maybe it was time for full-scale war against God. It was time he called his war council and planned an all-out war. This time he would not concentrate on the earth. He would strike at heaven and have Angel Michael and all the archangels hanged. As for God himself, it might not be easy to put an end to his supposedly everlasting life. He would simply cage him somewhere, like a canary, and make him watch Lucifer the conqueror rule over heaven, hell, and earth.

And that chap called Jesus, who had come from nowhere and superseded all of them. Michael was a fool, still playing the role of a small soldier while Jesus the parvenu was already much higher than him in status and even considered as the son of God. Jesus was not a soldier like Michael but certainly had to be handled with tact. While Michael would be in the battle front fighting, this Jew would surely introduce other, unconventional methods that might prove far more effective. It would certainly be necessary to keep a special eye on him when they launched a war against heaven.

Satan still had a small following in heaven, angels who were disappointed with the solemn atmosphere and needed some bustle and hustle in their lives. Some of these angels were actually spies, while the others were not quite sure of the life out there with Satan and did not want to take the risk of quitting. With a full-scale war, they would happily take sides with Satan.

But what of the earth? It was the coveted prize, and there was no way the war could be confined to heaven. With hell attacking, many of the battles would take place in heaven and spill over to the earth.

The next thing that came to Satan's mind was the constitution of this war council. A standard war council existed, but this was a special war. While the war would be going on in heaven, he would have people on earth preparing for the takeover. That is where he could use loyal followers like Bzinkem. During his first war with Michael, in which he ended up disgraced, fighting took place in heaven and then he was cast out. He had not thought of involving the people of the earth to support him. Now he would not make that same error.

Satan stood up from his chair and went to the window where he stood looking down at the earth for a while. It was really a coveted prize. A shrill whistling sound issued from his lips and three ghouls appeared from nowhere and floated to him.

"Yes, master," they said in quavering voices, "we are here to do your bidding."

"Summon my war council," Satan said. "Tell them we meet in an hour's time."

"Done master" the quavering voices answered "Done."

An hour in hell was ten days on earth.

In an hour's time, as ordered, Satan's courtroom was full of the vilest demons that had ever existed. On a high pedestal by Satan were Abaddon, who was Satan's assistant in Hell, Caym, the Grand President of Hell, Semiazas, the Chief of the Fallen Angels, and Lucifer's brother Baphomet. These tough looking leaders were always under close scrutiny from Satan as they were as ambitious as Satan to rule the world. By the side was a table occupied by Baalberith, who was the Chief Secretary of Hell. He had a bottle of blood that he used as ink and a vulture from which he constantly plucked off feathers to use as quill.

The next in rank were Adramelech, the Chancellor and President of the High Council of Devils; Baal, the Commanding General of the Infernal Armies and Azazel, the Standard Bearer of the Armies of Hell. They sat on stone chairs that were as cold as they themselves looked.

The commanding officers were all present and many of them were nobles and lords of high standing. There was a Prince of Hell called Balan, a Count of Hell called Raum who commanded thirty legions of demons, and a Count of Hell called Furfur who commanded twenty six legions of demons.

Other commanders of noble blood included, Aguares, the Grand Duke of Eastern Hell, who Commanded thirty legions of devils; Alocera Grand Duke of Hell, who commanded thirty-six legions of devils; Amduscas, a Grand Duke of Hell, who commanded twenty-nine legions of devils; Aym, a Grand Duke of Hell, who commanded twenty-six legions of demons and Andras, a Grand Duke of Hell, who commanded thirty legions of devils.

Some of the high ranking commanders were of ordinary blood but were still very powerful. They included Leviathan, the Grand Admiral of Hell; Buer, Commander of fifty legions of devils in Hell; Abigor, commander of sixty legions of devils; Ronwe, commander of nineteen legions of devils in Hell.

There were co-opted members to this war council, demons very close to Satan and thus very powerful. There was Valafar, a Grand Duke of Hell, Chax a Grand Duke of Hell and Orias, a Marquis of Hell.

Because of their specific functions, some demons were always invited to war council meetings. There was Astaroth, Grand Duke of Western Hell and Lord Treasurer; Nergal, the Chief of the Secret Police of Hell; Nybras, the Publicist of the Pleasures of Hell; Damas, the Ambassador of Hell for Russia, and Xaphan, the demon who stokes the furnaces of Hell when it gets too cold.

Apart from these master demons of Hell, there were six strangers to Hell sitting together on one side of Satan's throne room.

Satan looked round the large, cold room and was satisfied that all his commanders were present. They had never been engaged in any other war since they had faced inglorious defeat in front of God's armies. They were always plotting and planning but had never gathered the force to launch an actual war. This time, however, Satan was determined.

His determination was fuelled by his strong ambition for power over heaven and earth and his anger stemming from the constant disgrace he received from God's commanding officer. At the same time, he was comforted by the thought that God would never want to destroy him completely. He was a necessary evil; God needed him to give earthlings a reason to run to him for protection.

"Fellow demons," Satan said, opening the meeting, "this is our umpteenth war council meeting and all our previous meetings have always ended without any real decision to attack God. We have been concentrating on the earth and, no doubt, making some progress. But each time God sends that stooge of his called Michael to come and disgrace me. We must put a stop to that. "

"We agree with you," said Caym, the Grand President of Hell. "It is high time we do something about it. Our armies have been idle for too long. "

"The importance of this meeting cannot be overstated," Satan said. "That is why I commissioned our roving Ambassador to the earth, Thamuz, and Damas, Hell's Ambassador for Russia, to rally along these six senior fiends from the Earth. They are Grand Fiends representing the six continents on earth. You have Bzinkem from Africa, Tezcatlípoca from North America, Ravana from Asia, Po-Tangotango from Oceana, Pitkis from Europe, and Lebara from South America. They are led by Itzcoliuhqui, the Grand Baron. "

"You are all welcome to hell," said Abaddon, King of the Demons of Hell

"Thank you, sir," the Grand Fiends replied.

"Now," said Satan. "Let us move into the issue of the day. We have to carry out a full-scale war against heaven and take it down. The headquarters of the universe will become Hell after that. "

"And what do we do with God?" asked Semiazas, the Chief of the Fallen Angels.

"We can decide that when we have taken him captive," said Adramelech, Chancellor and President of the High Council of Devils.

"Our armies are prepared for war and we have been growing strong in numbers," said Baal, the Commanding General of the Infernal Armies.

"That is good to here," said Caym. "So what we need now is for our commanders to develop a watertight strategy that will guarantee our success. "

"We have to develop a good strategy and consider choice of weapons too. You see, our last real war against Michael's forces took place eons ago. At that time, a great general like Baalberith was comfortable using the trident as his weapon, and the great Abaddon fought with a mere spear. Since then, we have never trained in the use of modern weapons. "

"I am not sure Michael and his troops have improved upon their weapons either," said Abaddon.

"I don't know," Satan said, "but he has been using thunderbolts against me for a while. "

"We could start using those, too," said Damas. "That Greek called Zeus started the use of thunderbolts and, today, some African witch doctors have a crude form of it. "

"Before we come to weapons, how prepared are you to fight?" Satan asked.

"We are quite prepared to fight," said Baal. "Even without formal training, we are always ready. Give the order and we shall blast God and his followers out of heaven. "

"My chief has said the right thing," said Azazel, the Standard Bearer of the Armies of Hell. "All we need to do is rally the troops and that won't take much time. "

"What strategy do we use?" Satan asked.

"We march straight to heaven and take them by surprise," said Aym, a Grand Duke of Hell.

"I support what he has just said," said Andras, a Grand Duke of Hell. "If we use the element of surprise and strike

with absolute force, we shall certainly crush them like insects.
"

"We should not forget that we of hell are not allowed anywhere near heaven," said Astaroth, Grand Duke of Western Hell and Lord Treasurer. "How do we get in there before crushing them?"

"Those old angels have grown complacent and bored," said Leviathan, the Grand Admiral of Hell. "They have been drinking too much nectar, and I wonder whether heaven is still well guarded. "

"Heaven is there for us to take," Said Buer. "They have waited for us to attack for too long and have certainly concluded that we will never make up our minds to wage war. A surprise blitz war will be quite effective. "

"How I would love to see God's face when we put him in a cage and parade him around for all to see," Satan said wistfully. "And that Michael, I will hang him myself. "

"Everybody is for war," Abaddon said.

"Good," Satan said. "Now, let's listen to our servants from the earth. Out there, they are leaders and might have much to contribute. "

"Thank you, sir," said Itzcoliuhqui. "We are very grateful that you involved us in the ultimate war against God and heaven. My colleagues and I from the earth want at all cost to see Lucifer in full control, so we hope our little contributions will help in achieving this great goal. "

"After listening to the determination to fight and lay waste to heaven," said Bzinkem, "every demon on earth would be very satisfied that our bosses in hell are not taking things lying down. We are very happy for that. "

"That is well said," agreed Leviathan.

"However," continued Bzinkem, "I have a small worry that I wish to express. "

"Go ahead, my faithful servant," Satan said.

"God has not been sleeping all this while," Bzinkem said. "What are you saying?" shouted Buer. "I alone command fifty legions of devils and my other colleagues here command many other legions. What can those lazy bums in heaven do against us?"

"The war that is going on already does not concern armies, and the weapons used are not normal," Bzinkem said.

"What type of weapons are they?" said Nergal, the Chief of the Secret Police of Hell. "I could send my spies to go and investigate. "

"Well, there is this man called Jesus, who, though now in heaven, has a great influence on earth. He is actually doing much damage to the achievements of our master, Satan. God had already engaged you in war by using Jesus, but Jesus's battle ground is on earth. "

"You don't mean it. " Said Nergel

"He has of late invented a new but very effective weapon against us called Holy Ghost fire. "

"Is the fire as hot as what I produce in my furnaces?" asked Xaphan, the demon who stoked the furnaces of Hell.

"Your furnaces are nowhere near the force of this weapon," said Damas, Hell's Ambassador for Russia.

"We had been struggling to counter the destructive force of the name Jesus but had not yet succeeded when this weapon was developed, "said Bzinkem.

"So, just as we have mastered the art of hitting below the belt whenever the opportunity arises," said Satan, "God and his lackeys are also surfacing with war tactics that are not conventional?"

"That is just the situation," said Lebara, the Grand Fiend of South America. "Some of the weapons are outright ridiculous. You have stuff like rosaries and crucifixes, which they now used to fight us. "

"They even use water. They have what they call Holy water," said Po-Tangotango from Oceana.

"Would you imagine that they also use a collection of old stories to harass us?" Pitkis from Europe said.

"He means the bible," said Itzcoliuhqui, the Grand Baron. "The stories are all inside the Bible, and they use it to cast our demons out of our victims, to prevent us from taking victims, and to make us miserable. "

"Yes, I think I know how powerful that silly collection of old stories called the Bible can be if used by the right person," Nergel said.

"What we are saying here is that war against God could be quite complicated," said Itzcoliuhqui.

"In that case," said Amduscas, Grand Duke of Hell, "mere armies may find it very difficult. I am a soldier and I know what it means when you are facing an enemy whose weapons are not standard. "

"You may be aware of the force and fighting methods of God's army under Angel Michael," Bzinkem said, "but God has a bigger army made up of supposedly good people who died and are prepared to continue working for him. "

"You mean the Saints?" Damas asked.

"Yes," Bzinkem replied. "You see, when God has a good servant on earth, he makes much use of him even after death. "

"Saints are supposed to be people who lived exemplary lives while on earth, and are now supposed to be in heaven. " Satan said "However, as all of us here know, many of these supposedly good people were not actually that good while on earth and are rather in Hades with no access to Charon's boat that can ever take them back across the Styx. "

"Or in our armies," said Alocer, a Grand Duke of Hell. "Many of my soldiers are revered on earth as Saints. "

"What we should understand, therefore, is that God has been preparing for war already," said Pitkis. "In fact, war has been going on all along on earth. "

"What he is saying is quite true," Satan said. "While you people have been sitting out here in hell, raising huge armies of dead persons that did not follow the ways of God when they were alive, war has been going on on earth. I have virtually been fighting it alone with only these Grand Fiends as my Generals. "

Satan turned to the Grand Fiends.

"Do you have any concrete thing to propose?"

"I have a proposal to make," said Po-Tangotango, the Grand Fiend from Oceana. "Given the fact that the earth is the coveted prize, Heaven has been concentrating all its efforts there. All their new heavenly weapons are designed to work on earth, and most of them are different from the ordinary war weapons that you know. "

"So," said Amducas, "what exactly do you propose?"

"I propose that we forget about attacking heaven," said Pitkis. "Let us concentrate on earth. "

"Forget about attacking heaven?" Alocer asked. "With all our troops ready and poised to attack?"

"The idea is that if heaven is concentrating on the earth, then they have a good reason," said Itzcoliuhqui, the Grand

Baron. "If heaven is not bothered about hell, then they don't consider your armies as of any consequence. And it means they are aware of the fact that you can't defeat them. "

"I am seeing some sense in what he is saying," said Satan. "You need to go down to earth and see the kind of action that God is taking there. I have been working hard with my Grand Fiends, but we are outnumbered. Now, if all of you stopped brooding in your private abodes here in hell and followed me to earth with your armies, we would easily push God out. "

"May I specify here that the effort on earth will not depend on conventional warfare?" said Bzinkem. "Out there, there are strange soldiers using strange weapons. In Nigeria, for example, God just created a crack force whose members are known as Prayer Warriors. They are fast spreading all over Africa, and their weapon is Prayer. "

"Prayer?" asked Chax, a Grand Duke of Hell. "But that cannot be a weapon. I thought prayers consisted mainly of silly praises to God or continuous requests for one favour or another. "

"There you are wrong. Prayers have been developed into a powerful weapon against us. At times, they simply repeat the name, 'Jesus' several times and we are completely weakened. "

"That is why," Lebara said, "Hell's commanders shall need to be retrained to make them cope with the type of war that is going on earth. "

"You remember when we tried to introduce physical wars so that we could spread from Jesus' birth place to the rest of the world? Many of God's supporters went out on crusade. This shows their determination to support God. Now, with all the new approaches introduced, we have to work hard. "

"Working hard here does not mean that we have to bring in soldiers with ordinary weapons," said Itzcoliuhqui. "We need manpower, but those who will mostly use an artful tongue to wreak havoc. Generally, most of the moves shall be underground, with our troops all converted into false prophets and fake pastors."

"The strategy of using false prophets is predicted in their book, the Bible," said Bzinkem. "We have to come out with something stronger and attack on all fronts. While some are breaking up happy marriages by flirting with the husband or wife, others will be causing discord between members of the society."

"We shall need all of Hells armies on earth." said Itzcoliuhqui.

"Now, let us have a short break," Satan declared.

At this point, Dagon the Baker of Hell sent in pastries that were served round by several Succubus demons. The succubae were serving from marble trays while Incubus demons were serving bloody drinks. A choir of ghouls, banshees, and furies had been assembled to entertain the honourable guests, and some eerie music was being produced.

After short break, Satan called the meeting to order.

"We have listened to our Grand Fiends from the earth," he said, "and they have brought forward wonderful proposals. What has the war council got to say?"

"I think we should seriously consider what they have said," said Valafar. .

"The Grand Duke is right," said Orias, a Marquis of Hell. "Most of our commanders, constituting the bulk of this war council, have hardly been down to fight on earth. They have spent their time working out the possibility of a war against heaven and have never come up with any concrete move. We, on the other hand, who have been operating on earth, have achieved something. "

"I believe our secretary has records about our interventions on earth," Valafar said. "Please let our senior soldiers be informed. "

"Go on secretary," Satan said.

The secretary opened some strange record book, checked through, and turned to the meeting members.

"Actually, we have made several efforts on earth using the kind of unorthodox approaches that God himself uses," said Baalberith, who was the Chief Secretary of Hell. "We have come close to succeeding on several occasions, but God always ended up having the upper hand. "

"The activities the secretary is referring to have cost us a lot, and we have the financial records here," said Astaroth, Grand Duke of Western Hell and Lord Treasurer.

"List out the activities then," said Nybras, the Publicist of the Pleasures of Hell, "so that we can improve upon them or use them to come out with new approaches. "

"Let's listen then," the secretary said. "We penetrated all the inhabitants of the world at one time and made them all very evil. We succeeded in turning all of them against God. "

"The whole world?" asked Abigor.

"Yes," said Satan. "It is just that you soldiers were not involved in this. Continue Berith. "

"Our manipulation over the people was quite great, pushing God to decide to punish all of them," Baalberith said. "That would have been an end to God's world. We could have then brought in Satan's world. "Baalberithtokk a sip of crocodile tears from a horny cup and continued

Unfortunately for us, out of the whole world, there was one good man and his family. While the rest of the world perished in a great flood, this one good man and his family were saved by God, and he started building a new, good world from scratch. "

"All our efforts and money was lost," said Astaroth the Treasurer.

"Shortly after that, however," continued the Secretary, "We succeeded in convincing the people to build a tower that would link them to heaven. We hoped that they would carry the evil ways we had already instilled in them right to heaven. They were making good progress when God confused their languages and they ended up destroying the project. "

"God has not been having it easy then," said Ronwe. "Certainly not," said the secretary. "Failing to mount a successful global strategy, It was decided that, instead of a global attack, we should cut off small sectors and destroy them completely before moving to another. We started with Sodom and Gomorrah and transformed these two cities into centres of evil, sin, and all sorts of crimes against God. This was going to be our base on earth. But God rushed in and burnt all the inhabitants of the two cities before their bad influence could be taken everywhere. "

"As we have been making all these moves," Satan said, "God too has not been sleeping. "

"We achieved most of these feats without hell's armies, however," said Astaroth, "so the proposal that we concentrate all forces on earth could be very helpful. "

"But our troops are quite sizable. We have many legions to move to earth. Where shall we keep them?" asked Buer,

"That is quite easy," said Satan. "The earthlings already believe that we live everywhere on earth. We inhabit volcanoes, hills, and caves. They believe that we infest all their streams and rivers, lakes and seas, and even the oceans. Every shady grove or frightening-looking place is considered as our abode. Some time ago, I even heard some of them claiming that I reside in Cleg four, where ever this ridiculous place is. All we need to do is truly inhabit these places, from which our forces will come out each time to carry out their mission. "

"What the Lord Satan is saying, these are some of the tactics we will have to rely on," said Bzinkem. "In Africa, we already use the elements in nature as one of our main forms of penetrating humans. We have already made people to believe strongly in the existence of air, water, and, the most feared, fire spirits. The most popular among them, however, are the water spirits. They are supposed to be lodged in virtually every existing body of water, be it a stream, a river, a waterfall and rapids, a lake, the sea, or even the oceans. It is generally believed that Lord Satan controls all these natural features. "

"Back in the days of ancient Greece and Rome, we used Poseidon and Saturn to control all these, but at one point they started becoming too human," said Leviathan, the Grand Admiral of Hell. "As a result, our control of the oceans and seas faded. We shall need to reinforce that aspect. "

"Now," said Abaddon, "to actually destabilize God's control over the earth, what do we exploit? What elements do we use to make the people go completely astray and provoke God's anger?"

"There are aspects that we have been exploiting already to get followers of Satan, but this is at a smaller level," said Bzinkem. "God has allowed a lot of unfairness on earth and given people the free will to exercise their greed and covetous

103

attitudes. Yes, with a bit of convincing, many people on earth would be prepared to sacrifice their family for wealth. "

"On the other hand," said Lebara, "the unfairness on earth is startling. God gives talents to certain people and deprives others of any. Even those with talents do not benefit equally. God gives the opportunity to exploit these talents to a few. These few make in one day more money than others make in a life's time. There are yet another group of earthlings that are simply born into wealth and juicy opportunities. From little or no effort of theirs, they find themselves controlling wealth that a whole city could have thrived on satisfactorily. Such unjustly wealthy fellows often end up arrogant and vain. Apart from wealth, others have power and use it to do what they want. This has left the belief in God rather wanting in certain parts of the world. "

"In many parts of the world, these unfairly rich persons now take God for granted so we can easily penetrate them," said Itzcoliuhqui. "Those with average incomes are still kind of fervent, while the very poor are giving up after having been deceived for too long that it was much less difficult for a camel to pass through the eye of a needle than for a rich man to go to heaven. We have many possible ways to use Hell's armies to capture the world away from God. "

"Is the war council now convinced that we should concentrate all our efforts on earth?" Satan asked.

"We have valiant soldiers that have been straining on the leash to take on God's army and crush it," said Baal, the Commanding General of the Infernal Armies. "We can't go wasting time looking for silly approaches that do not involve force and violence. Let us strike directly. "

"I, too, believe in outright war," said Balan, a prince of hell. "We should use force. "

"I understand your point of view," said Caym, the Grand President of Hell. "You are soldiers and soldiers always want to fight. But then soldiers always have politicians to control them and politicians always look for the easiest way out. What we have discussed here at length is quite important and far less explosive than outright war. I am sure Semiazas is of the same opinion?"

"Of course," said Semiazas, the Chief of the Fallen Angels. "Our fall from heaven was mighty and painful indeed. If we face them directly, we may land back with another very heavy thud. Let us penetrate like termites, and, before they know what is coming, we will have already taken over the earth. With the earth in our hands heaven will have no place. "

"We have all agreed" said Satan, "that we follow the advice of our Grand Fiends on earth and infiltrate every activity, every social strata, and just everything. We shall penetrate religion, sports, culture, health, education, leisure, industry, agriculture and…. "

"Please, give some explanations," Balberith said.

"Explanations? roared Satan. "What explanations do you need when everything is so clear? Bzinkem, explain to him. "

"In religion, for example, we bring in false prophets," said Bzinkem. "In sports, we corrupt all the referees and promote match-fixing. In health, we encourage fake drugs and fake healers. In culture and leisure, we encourage erotic and sexual activities. In education and sciences, we tactfully sneak in courses on devil worship in all school and university programs. "

Bzinkem stopped and looked at Satan to confirm whether he was on the right track.

"Continue," encouraged Satan.

"God made the error of giving the people of the earth free will and at the same time allowing certain aberrations or mutations that take a few of them off the standard and good life track. For example, it is a sin to kill or make other people suffer. Stealing is a sin. Fornication, homosexuality, and activities of perverts are all considered as sins. However, some people are born with these characteristics in them. They are either born vicious like Ivan the Terrible of Russia, kleptomaniacs, nymphomaniacs, or with homosexual tendencies. These people end up committing sins regularly whether they like it or not. All we need to do is to intensify such occurrences and get more than half the world living like maniacs, oversexed perverts, and full of angry tantrums. "

"That is something like it," Satan cut in. "Now, let the earth wait for us. We are coming with renewed force and confidence. "

In Heaven God smiled as he watched the war council meeting in Hell and noted their resolutions and new strategy. Although heaven was blocked from Hell, whatever transpired in hell could easily be watched from Heaven.

"I am the lord, your God. " He said "Thou shall not have another God but me. "

God's voice sounded quite loud among the gathering of Demons in hell and they all cringed in fear as Satan struggled to block his ear from the offending announcement. God looked around triumphantly. He had shown Hell's leaders that he was above them and still in control of the world. He now turned to his companions who were watching the scene in hell with him.

"Those fools in Hell will never realize that Jesus is me," he said to Saint Peter.

"They find it hard to believe that you could actually go down to the world and live there as a human," Saint Peter said. "Even us who were recruited by Jesus as his closest assistants, never found it easy to understand the relationship between God the Father and God the Son. "'Satan might have quite a following on earth but to get each person, he has to do a lot of nasty work and offer ill-gotten wealth and an easy life. Only lazy and greedy men fall for that. "

"But the earth is full of lazy and greedy men. " Saint Paul said

"I think you are being too lenient with Satan," said Saint Peter. "Left to me, we should not allow him to have access to the people of the earth. "

"You see, Peter," God said. "The people who are for me prove that they are really for me by making sacrifices. They fast once in a while, avoid bad and evil things, and deprive themselves of certain luxuries of life. Whether they call me God or Allah, it does not matter. The fact is that they revere me and await their reward in Heaven. "

"But Satan may end up getting most of the people of the world to his side," protested Saint Peter. "Most earthlings are weak and lust for the pleasures of the flesh, which Satan readily provides. We have to be careful. Don't forget that even many of your clergy men are quite vulnerable. "

"Peter!" God said "Where is your faith? You know very well that I am God almighty and always have the last word. I know why I gave free will to people of the earth and I know when to step in.

I am sorry lord, but there is so much evil on earth and that is what Satan wants. "Saint Peter said.

"Evil, Peter" said God "is a word that could be used loosely but which in certain situations may not carry the same impact. "

"How?" asked Saint Paul

"You see," God said "an Inca or Aztec priest that was born and made to understand that his role and duty to his people was to conduct human sacrifices is doing evil, but does not realize that what he is doing is wrong. "

"That sounds kind of odd. " said Saint Peter.

"May be. " replied God "Consider a child born into a tribe of cannibals who grows up as a cannibal and kills people to have his regular meals. "

"I see some sense in that. " Saint Paul said.

"Or one of those maniacs that come along through errors of creation. I do my best as God but nature allows certain errors to slip through. "

"We have understood that since we started working with you. " Saint Paul said.

"Now," God said "If one of those maniacs goes to the excess of nymphomania, steals even from beggars, or enjoys torturing others, he is simply responding to nature and nature is me. "

"If I understand you well lord," said Saint Paul "he cannot be fully blamed for evil that stems from nature. In this case, there was no free will. "

"You have understood it well Paul. "God said "For Evil to carry full blame, the perpetrator must be fully conscious of what he is doing and must be fully aware that what he is doing is wrong. Besides, he must not be compelled by any force or influence what so ever. Kleptomaniacs cannot hold back from stealing. Nymphomaniacs cannot hold back from fornication and adultery, and so on.

"You are getting us confused, Lord" Saint Peter said.

"You are disappointing me, Peter. " God said "You are supposed to be the leader of my troops against this new war that Satan is planning.

"I am almost failing you again lord. " Saint Peter replied "But with Paul by my side, nothing can stand in our way.

"Fine. " God said "So, what is our motto?"

"Kick the Devil out of the earth" said Saint Paul "and lock him up in Hell. "

"I wish we could circulate that all over the earth and make it work. " Said Jesus Christ wistfully.